"Thank you f... enjoyed it!"

"I enjoyed it, too." Bryant's blue eyes looked into hers and it was suddenly hard to breathe. They mesmerized her, drawing her nearer. Zoe felt his arms surround her and then his mouth was on hers—warm and urgent.

A soft moan escaped her as finally, reluctantly, he released her mouth.

"I think," Bryant said slowly, "something is going on between us."

Ever since KAREN VAN DER ZEE was a child growing up in Holland she wanted to do two things: write books and travel. She's been very lucky. Her American husband's work as a development economist has taken them to many exotic locations. They were married in Kenya, had their first daughter in Ghana and their second in the United States. They spent two fascinating years in Indonesia. Since then they've added a son to the family, as well. They've recently moved from Israel back to Ghana—but not permanently!

KAREN VAN DER ZEE

Fire and Spice

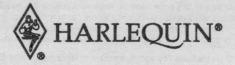

HARLEQUIN®

TORONTO • NEW YORK • LONDON
AMSTERDAM • PARIS • SYDNEY • HAMBURG
STOCKHOLM • ATHENS • TOKYO • MILAN • MADRID
PRAGUE • WARSAW • BUDAPEST • AUCKLAND

ISBN 0-373-18706-8

FIRE AND SPICE

First North American Publication 1999.

Copyright © 1995 by Karen van der Zee.

All rights reserved. Except for use in any review, the reproduction or
utilization of this work in whole or in part in any form by any electronic,
mechanical or other means, now known or hereafter invented, including
xerography, photocopying and recording, or in any information storage
or retrieval system, is forbidden without the written permission of the
publisher, Harlequin Enterprises Limited, 225 Duncan Mill Road,
Don Mills, Ontario, Canada M3B 3K9.

All characters in this book have no existence outside the imagination of
the author and have no relation whatsoever to anyone bearing the same
name or names. They are not even distantly inspired by any individual
known or unknown to the author, and all incidents are pure invention.

This edition published by arrangement with Harlequin Books S.A.

® and TM are trademarks of the publisher. Trademarks indicated with
® are registered in the United States Patent and Trademark Office, the
Canadian Trade Marks Office and in other countries.

Printed in U.S.A.

CHAPTER ONE

ZOE restlessly straightened the papers on her desk, then glanced at her watch. He would be here soon. She took a deep breath, letting her eyes slide over the information in the open file folder in front of her, information she could recite word for word. Well, almost. She fussed with her hair and moistened her lips. She was not nervous. Of course she was not nervous. This was a routine conference between school counselor and the parent of a student. She did it all the time. She was fully prepared, fully confident. Her hair this morning was cooperating, curling nicely rather than too exuberantly as it sometimes did. Her career suit was feminine yet professional. Looking in the mirror these days she still had a hard time recognizing herself.

According to the file, Mr Bryant Sinclair was a single parent, father of twelve-year-old Paul. No mention was made of a mother. He had a high position in a multinational corporation and had recently relocated from Argentina to Washington D.C. He had relocated straight into the first-floor apartment of the old historic town house where Zoe herself had recently moved in as well, on the second floor. This summer she had returned to Washington from Africa, where she'd lived for the past six years—two in Tanzania, one in Mauritania, three in Cameroon.

Mr Sinclair was a good-looking man, tall with big

shoulders and piercing blue eyes in a tanned face. He had thick blond hair and an uncompromisingly square chin and there was an aura of self-confidence and command about him. Not the kind of man who skipped your attention.

They'd met in passing, at the front door. They'd introduced themselves as polite people who shared a building did. He'd looked at her with a smile and she'd felt her heart turn over—not once, but twice at least. Instant combustion. There'd been no reason for it except something like love at first sight, or chemistry, or some lovely fantasy like that. Something very elemental, something outside of reason or logic, had happened.

And this whatever-it-was thing that had transpired between them was, of course, why she was sitting here at her desk in her small office at the Olympia International School with her heart in her throat waiting for him to come through the door.

It was not a positive situation she was going to have to discuss with him, which was very unfortunate. Mr Sinclair's son was flunking in a big way. Four weeks into the school year and he had collected an impressive string of zeros in every teacher's grade book. Zeros for not doing his work and not handing in assignments. Zoe sighed. Her unhappy task was to inform Mr Sinclair that there was a problem with his one and only son. Parents didn't like to hear that sort of thing. She didn't like much having to tell him.

At eight o'clock sharp he appeared in her open door, tall and imposing. Intense blue eyes settled on her face. 'Good morning,' he said, his voice deep and very masculine. It was a wonderful voice, the kind that stroked all your nerve-endings and made your blood sing.

Words stuck in her throat momentarily as she took in

the immaculate business suit, the pale blue shirt, the fashionable tie. The man knew how to dress. The man knew how to carry himself. The man knew how to look at a woman.

Having swallowed repeatedly, Zoe was able to return the greeting and ask him to come in. She stood up from her chair and held out her hand. His grasp was hard and warm and sent an electric shiver through her. A faint masculine scent of soap and aftershave reached her nostrils. It was eight in the morning and he was straight out of the shower, no doubt. Am image of the naked man with water pouring all over his tanned, muscled body flitted through her mind. Good lord, what was the matter with her? She didn't generally picture fully clothed man in front of her standing naked in the shower.

He released her hand and sat down, pulling up his trouser legs a little as he did so. His black shoes gleamed impressively. She'd seen other men in expensive clothes and shiny shoes in her office the last few weeks. Nothing had happened to her heartbeat. Nothing had curled around in her blood. Nothing had shivered up her spine. No disturbing images had come to mind. In short, these men had not disturbed her one bit. This one did. In a big way.

There was something intriguing about this man, something that didn't quite make sense. Why did a man like Mr Sinclair move into a simple, rented apartment? It was a nice apartment, to be true, located in a nice historic neighborhood, yet a man of his professional background would own a house or a luxury condominium. She'd noticed expensive cars in front of their building, emitting people who looked as if their clothes had come straight from Paris or Rome.

'I understand you wanted to discuss Paul's school performance,' he stated, observing her calmly.

Zoe folded her arms on the desk. 'Yes.' She took a deep breath. Suddenly it was difficult to focus on the issue at hand.

She'd had a chance to meet Paul and speak to him before school started, out in front of the house. He was a handsome boy, a little small for his age, with curly brown hair and blue-gray eyes that lacked the bright intensity of his father's, but instead held a touching vulnerability. For no particular reason she had felt drawn to him. When they'd first met, he'd been friendly and open with her, but once in school he'd clammed up when she'd talked to him.

'Your son is a likeable boy, Mr Sinclair, and obviously very intelligent.' To her relief, her voice sounded calm and professional.

He gave a half-smile. 'I know that.'

She glanced down at the file. 'I understand that you lived in Buenos Aires the past five years and that your son attended the international school there.'

He inclined his head fractionally. 'Correct.'

'I suppose he finds living in the States quite a change,' she said carefully. The school was full of children from many nations who had moved around from one country to another—children of parents employed by the United States government, foreign embassies and international agencies and companies. Students often had to make great adjustments.

'Yes.' He frowned slightly. 'Is there a problem, Ms Langdon?' His tone indicated that he wanted to make short of the preliminaries.

'As a matter of fact, yes, there is.' She looked straight at him, noticing with some separate part of her brain the strong line of his jaw, the straight nose, the well-chiseled mouth. 'To come straight to the point, Mr Sinclair, his interim report shows failing grades for all academic subjects. The report was sent home with Paul for your signature this week.'

'I didn't see it.'

She was not surprised. Paul had probably found it prudent not to show it to his father. Zoe handed him a copy from her file. He glanced at it and frowned. 'Are you sure this is correct?'

'Yes, I am. I've spoken to all his teachers. Paul's academic record suggests this is a very unusual situation. He is intelligent and has no learning disability and his grades in the past have been excellent.'

He nodded. 'Yes. So what is the problem?'

'Your son does not hand in most of his homework assignments and does not study or read as instructed. I have talked to him and he seems not at all interested in putting forth any effort.'

A short silence followed her words. 'I think they call this rebellion,' he said then, his voice even.

'I think it's more than that. Frankly, Mr Sinclair, I am concerned about him.'

His brows arched. 'Concerned? What exactly do you mean?'

He shows signs of being depressed, she wanted to say, but thought better of it. 'I've spoken to him on a couple of occasions and he seems withdrawn and uncommunicative. According to the comments of the teachers from his school in Argentina this is not his nature. Obviously something is bothering him. Something is not right.'

His blue eyes held hers. 'I think you're over-reacting,' he said lightly. 'He's been in school a mere four weeks. Isn't that a little soon to come to a diagnosis?'

Why did she feel defensive? 'I've not given a diagnosis. I simply stated that I think there's a problem. The sooner we identify a problem, the easier it is to deal with it.' She didn't like his casual attitude. She didn't like the tone of his voice.

He tapped his fingers on the chair's arm-rest. 'We've only just returned to the States, Ms Langdon. He needs time to adjust to a new environment. He's only been in school a few weeks.'

'Yes, of course.' There was no doubting the truth of that statement, yet she sensed quite clearly that there was more to it than an adjustment problem. It bothered her that the man seemed so unconcerned. 'Has he said anything about school?'

'Nothing except that his school in Argentina was much better and the teachers much nicer.' His mouth curved in amusement. 'Everything else is just fine, he has me believe.'

Everything was not fine. It was not normal for a happy, active, intelligent child suddenly to turn into a withdrawn kid who didn't do any school work and showed no enthusiasm for anything.

'Have you spoken to your son about his school work?'

'He told me he was not having problems with anything, and I assumed it was true. I've never had to be on his back to do his work; he was always very responsible about it.'

'But he isn't now.'

'So it appears,' he said lightly.

So it *is*, she corrected silently. Hadn't he noticed? Hadn't he paid any attention? How could a father not notice that his son was never doing any school work?

'He does not bring in his assignments,' she said evenly. 'He does not participate in class. He did not take up soccer. He's a very good soccer player, it says in his files.'

'Right. I expect he'll come around when he realizes he's only punishing himself. He's a proud kid and my bet is that he's not going to like the looks of those bad grades for very long. He'll get himself together, study ferociously and get all caught up.'

'Would you mind if I asked you a few more questions?'

He glanced at his watch. 'I don't have much time.'

Anger rushed to her head. This is about your son! she wanted to say. You have to have time!

She knew other parents, parents who had no time for their children, or had no interest in their lives. She would notice this with a sort of clinical detachment, feeling sorry for the child, disapprove of the parents, but that was where it stopped. As a professional her duty was to help if she could, but it was not good to get too emotionally involved with these situations. The anger she was feeling now was not very professional. She looked back down at her hands folded on the desk and collected herself. She felt her heart race. 'Is there any problem at home that might cause him to feel unhappy?'

His silence was intentional. 'No, there is no problem at home, Ms Langdon.' In spite of his casual tone, she sensed a distinct chill in him. Stay out of my business, the subtle message was.

Nerves began to jump inside her, but she refused to let it show. 'Did Paul want to come back to the States?'

He shrugged. 'There was no choice.'

It was not an answer to her question. 'Choice or no choice, did he want to leave Argentina?'

'No. I thing that's why he's rebelling now. I don't

expect it to last long. He'll settle in soon enough. He'll make friends.'

She nodded, hoping he would be right, fearing he was not.

He came to his feet. 'With all due respect, Ms Langdon, please do not make too much of this. A month is not very long.' He smiled. 'I don't believe it's time for panic and in-depth psychoanalysis just yet.' The tone of his voice was polite, but held a faint imperious note. It infuriated her. Obviously, talking with him any further would not be productive. He had pressing matters at the office. What was the matter with this man? Why wasn't he worried? Still, it would not do to antagonize him. What she needed was cooperation.

She stood up as well. 'Let's hope things will turn out all right,' she said lightly, proud of her own cool control. 'Please give me a call if there's anything I can help with, Mr Sinclair.' He probably wouldn't, but the offer was automatic. 'That's what I'm here for.'

'Thank you.' He looked straight at her and suddenly, amazingly, he smiled broadly and humor sparked in his eyes. 'Perhaps we can dispense with the formalities. We are neighbors, after all. Call me Bryant.'

Was this a peace offering? Well, what could she say? No, thank you, I'd rather call you Mr?

She nodded politely. 'Thank you, and I'm Zoe.'

He gave a little nod, his eyes a brilliant blue as they held hers. 'See you, Zoe.'

She closed the door behind his broad back and sat down again in her chair behind the desk, letting out a deep sigh.

She didn't like this man. She didn't like his casual

attitude, the faint arrogance in his voice. She didn't like those blue eyes.

She didn't like the way he smiled at her.

Yes, she did.

She groaned and dropped her head on the desk.

CHAPTER TWO

ALL through the day Zoe kept thinking of Bryant Sinclair, seeing his blue eyes, aware of the warm feeling curling around in her stomach. Yet other, conflicting thoughts fought for attention—a father denying there might be a problem with his son, a father obviously not wanting to take it seriously and discuss it. She didn't like it. She didn't like it one bit.

It was not going to be easy. Yet she was determined to try to help Paul. It was her job. And there was something about the boy, the vulnerable look in his eyes, that touched her.

She had lunch with a couple of teachers and the bubbly school secretary, who was a consummate gossip. Ann had her very own plug into the Washington grapevine.

Ann had noticed Bryant leave Zoe's office that morning. She knew his address and she knew who he was and she was eager to tell all. Bryant Sinclair came from a wealthy family who owned the international corporation for which he worked, according to the school files. He'd headed up large projects in various places around the world, most recently in Argentina. Some business magazine—Ann couldn't remember which—had done an article on Bryant and the projects he'd managed. He had been married once, years ago, but what had happened to his wife nobody knew.

Various possibilities were offered. Zoe listened and said nothing, chewing her sandwich.

The other puzzle discussed was the reason why a man like Bryant Sinclair would live in a rented apartment, be it a nice one. And wasn't it Zoe's good fortune to live in the same building? Imagine the possibilities!

'Have you been inside his place?' Ann asked Zoe, her eyes wide and eager.

Zoe said no and asked if anyone wanted more coffee. She was not comfortable discussing Bryant Sinclair, although, if she were honest with herself, she'd have to admit to being curious like crazy.

By the time she locked her office at four, she was more then ready to go home. It was a long but pleasant walk back to her apartment and the air was still full of late summer warmth. Chrysanthemums bloomed in a glowing array of warm autumn colors in the small city gardens and in pots arranged along stone steps. She hadn't been home during the fall for years and she'd forgotten how beautiful they were.

She had not yet purchased a car and so far she had managed without one, walking and using the Metro or taxis for longer distances. Maybe she could wait till spring, when it would be nice to be able to get out into the countryside.

She stopped at the bakery and bought some dark, crusty bread. A young woman with a new-born baby in her arms was looking longingly at the apple strudel. Zoe peered into the tiny, sleeping face, feeling overwhelmed with sudden longing. She wanted a baby, to hold close and to love. She wanted a man, to hold close and to love. Preferably first the man, then the baby, she thought wryly as she moved on down the street hugging her purchases to her chest. She was twenty-nine. It was per-

fectly normal to want these things. She intended to be a
great wife and a super-cool mom. She grinned at herself.
A lot easier said than done, but she was ready for the
challenge. Sometimes she felt as if she would burst with
the need to give her love—as if she carried inside her a
large supply that would overflow if she didn't dispense
it.

You are nuts, she told herself, and put thoughts of
loving and bursting out of her mind.

Reaching the town house, she skipped up the stone
steps to the front door and opened it. Inside the
entryway she checked her mail. There was a letter from
Nick, which gave her a jolt of pleasure, and she rushed
up the stairs to her apartment, eager to read it. She made
a pot of tea, changed out of her suit into jeans and a
T-shirt, and plunked herself on the sofa with the letter.

Nick was a science teacher at the boarding-school in
Cameroon where she had worked for three years herself.
He told her of the people she knew—the couple that had
married in a lavish tribal ceremony, the latest news of
the students and the teachers, the herbalist who had
cured the pain in his foot with a magic potion, the
Spanish cultural attaché he loved.

My Spanish princess has forsaken me for another. How
dare she? you may ask. Actually, I think she wanted a
prince. I am not a prince; I am from New Jersey. None
the less I am devastated. Loneliness creeps in every nook
and cranny of my existence. Why did you have to leave,
Zoe? You were my best friend. You should have been
here to comfort me in my time of distress.

What am I to do? I spend my nights in isolation, unless Jacob comes by with palm wine and then we sit and

discuss the cassava harvest and the mysteries of the female psyche and I drink too much and become very undignified, which I sincerely regret the next morning. Loneliness is a devastating condition, possibly terminal. I so long for your lethal chocolate-chip coconut cookies and your riveting conversation, but your house stands empty when I, ever hopeful of a miracle, pass by.

We all miss you. We miss your house and the comfort and friendship we found within its crooked walls, not to speak of the culinary delights. Your house was a haven of domesticity in this land of deprivation.

Needless to say, I ask myself daily why I am still here, turning grayer every day. Why I stay in this godforsaken dusty little African town. The reason is that I like it.

I so hope you are happy in your swishy apartment in the nation's capital. In moments of despair I soothe myself trying to visualize it: lots of plants. Lovely flowered teacups. A cozy wood fire on cold nights. The heavenly aroma of something baking in the oven.

I hope you find what you're looking for, Zoe. I can see you already in my mind's eye, sitting on a sofa, a handsome husband by your side, a baby on your lap with your lovely big brown eyes and warm smile. How serene an image!

Sometimes I wonder if I'll spend the rest of my life here in Africa, growing little by little into a mad eccentric…

Zoe laughed out loud. Nick was an eccentric already. He was forty years old, had never been married and had lived all over the world, settling here and there for a few years to teach or do other work that seemed interesting.

And she, of course, had been heading the same direction—straight into mad eccentricity. One steamy night she'd woken in a cold sweat and seen the warning written on the ceiling: Go home! Be normal!

Zoe picked up the pretty flowered teapot and refilled her cup. Sipping at the hot, strong tea, she finished the letter. Poor Nick. All alone in a small African town.

Poor me, she thought suddenly, all alone in a big American town. She grimaced. 'Oh, stop it,' she muttered out loud. After all, this was what she had wanted—to come back to the States, settle down and grow some roots. Growing roots. It called up images of flourishing, large-leaved plants flowering luxuriantly and spreading sweet perfume. It was a lovely vision and it made her smile.

Putting Nick's letter on the table, she came to her feet and wandered around the small apartment. It was a lovely place with solid oak doors and hardwood floors dating back a hundred and fifty years. She stood in front of the window which had a view of a narrow, tree-lined street of other historic town houses with gabled roofs and wrought-iron railings along the front steps.

Bryant Sinclair's silver-blue Saab was not in its parking place in front of the house, she noticed automatically, aware suddenly that she was always noticing his car—or its absence. You're like a busybody old lady spying on her neighbors, she told herself. Don't you have anything more productive to do?

It was too early for Bryant to be home. Mrs Garcia, the housekeeper, would be in the apartment keeping Paul company until his father came home. She wondered what the place looked like.

There'd be expensive furniture, no doubt, but she could not quite imagine what it might look like, which was not surprising—she didn't know the man.

She had, however, a very clear picture of the man

himself in her mind—the blond hair, the blue, blue eyes, that prominent chin. Just thinking of him made her pulse do funny things.

Turning away from the window, she glanced around the room and pushed the image of those blue eyes out of her head.

She'd furnished and decorated her apartment herself and she was happy with the result. Everything was perfect, everything in its place. Everything cozy and comfortable. It had taken her a lot of effort and energy to get it the way she wanted it, arranging her eclectic assortment of paintings, woven wall-hangings, wood carvings and baskets in such a way as to make it a unified whole.

This was her nest and she loved the warmth and coziness of it, the color and brightness. She was going to be happy here in her new life. Washington was an exciting city with all sorts of cultural entertainments—plays, concerts, lectures, seminars—all those things she had missed in the last few years.

She put on a tape of cheery reggae and began preparing a salad with lettuce, avocado and goat cheese. She ate it at the small table, along with a slice of the German bread and a glass of wine. It was delicious.

It was pathetic. She was alone, eating alone. What good was all this without someone to share it with? Suddenly she longed to be back in Africa, in her shabby little house in the dusty town, eating with friends—some starchy yam and oily fish soup—anything. She longed for friends around her, conversation, laughter. She longed for the sense of community, the sharing and support.

Loneliness overwhelmed her and her salad blurred in front of her eyes, the colors swirling together in pretty shades of green and white. Angry with herself, she blinked to clear her eyes. She was not going to get maudlin and weep into her salad like some tragic heroine. This was stupid, stupid. She couldn't allow herself to give in to these feelings. She would make friends here, build a new life. It would just take some time and effort.

The phone rang.

'Hi, it's me, Maxie,' said the voice. Maxie lived in the town house next door, a large, beautiful place which she shared with her bald husband, several exotic caged birds, and a boa constrictor. She had a mass of bright red hair, a sexy voice and a body to kill for. She wore the wildest, most flamboyant clothes Zoe had ever seen.

'Hi,' said Zoe. When she'd moved in, on an excruciatingly hot August day, Maxie had offered lemonade, the use of her telephone, and a view of her snake. They'd talked briefly on occasion afterward. Maxie and her husband Derek owned a very exclusive international art shop and made frequent buying trips overseas.

'We're having our annual end-of-summer party on Saturday,' said Maxie. 'I'd like you to come.'

A party! People! Conversation! It was an omen. Zoe felt her spirits soar heavenward.

'Oh, thank you! I'd love to. Can I bring something?'

'I'm having it catered. It's a big party, lots of people, and I don't want to bother with the food. How have you been?'

'I like the school and the staff, but I'm still readjusting to things American, like overloaded supermarkets with fifteen brands of everything and phones that work and semi-sane traffic.'

Maxie laughed her husky laugh. 'You'll find some soul mates at the party. Lots of globe-trotters and foreign types.'

'Sounds interesting. What do I wear?'

'Anything you like. There'll be people in jeans and saris and dashikis and bow-tie, so whatever.'

'Good. When you mentioned catering I was worried I had to get something long with sequins or feathers.'

'Oh, please, spare me!' Maxie laughed. 'Well, I'll see you Saturday, then, eight.'

Zoe replaced the receiver and grinned to herself. She felt suddenly very light and not at all depressed any more. The invitation was an omen. A definite omen that exciting things were lurking around the corner. She took several dance steps back to the table to finish her salad.

Afterward she felt too restless to read or watch television. She needed something to do. She glanced around the tiny kitchen, looking for inspiration. She should bake something time-consuming and elaborate. A cake. A luscious, decadent chocolate cake with nuts. She'd take it to school tomorrow and leave it in the teachers' lounge. It wouldn't last long there.

She was two eggs short. Well, the corner store was still open. Grabbing her purse, she rushed out the door, down the stairs to the hall. Opening the front door, she found herself face to face with Bryant Sinclair. No, not face to face. He was quite a bit taller than she. Her heart lurched as she looked up at him, meeting his blue, blue eyes. Like a summer sky, came the sudden thought. Apparently he was just returning from work. He wore the suit he had worn that morning, a briefcase in one hand, keys dangling in the other.

'Thank you,' he said, giving a vague smile.

She was aware suddenly that she was gaping at him stupidly. She rearranged her face in what she hoped was a more dignified expression. 'I was just going out for

some eggs.' Now why did she tell him that? There was
no reason to explain herself.

Amusement gleamed in his eyes. 'May your quest be
successful,' he said, 'otherwise drop by and have some
of mine. On second thought, why not just have some of
mine right now and save yourself the trip?'

'Thank you, but I need the exercise and I'm sure they
have some at the corner store.' She scooted down the
steps to the brick sidewalk and heard the front door close
behind her. Her heart was going crazy. What was the
matter with her? The moment she saw him, her senses
went wild. This was not normal, was it? After all, she
didn't even like the man.

Bryant was watching her. It was odd—she could feel his
eyes on her like a touch on her skin. Zoe sipped her
wine as she slowly turned and allowed her gaze to pass
casually over Bryant, pretending she didn't notice him.
He was talking to an Arab in a white flowing robe and
a woman in a bunny costume. There was indeed an intriguing array of clothes. She glanced around Maxie's
crowded living-room, glimpsing a man in a dashiki, two
women in saris and an assortment of exotic print shirts.
The rest of the guests wore a more standard variety of
party garb, including Bryant, who sported dark trousers
and a blue and black print silk shirt, open at the neck.

She wore a short little party dress with off-the-
shoulder sleeves that she had bought in Rome when
she'd visited her mother there this summer on her way
back to the States. It was black and sexy, and actually
she felt a bit naked in it, although the dress did not
expose anything that shouldn't be exposed in polite company. It was just that she hadn't worn this sort of clothes
for ages.

Arriving at the party a few minutes ago, she'd been surprised to see Bryant, then realized that he was Maxie's neighbor as much as she. A moment later he was standing in front of her, apparently having shed the Arab and the bunny. 'You look rather lost,' he said.

She grimaced. 'I don't know anyone here. I suppose I should just dive in and introduce myself to someone who looks interesting and start a conversation.'

He surveyed the room. 'Who looks interesting to you?'

'The sheik over there, the one you were just talking to. I can just see him on a camel trotting through the desert.'

He took a sip from his drink. 'You find that idea romantic?'

'I said interesting, not romantic,' she said, giving him a challenging look which he pretended not to notice.

'I'm afraid you're going to be disappointed,' he said. 'The man was born and bred in Texas. Spent several years in Saudi Arabia with an oil company, and now shows up at parties in his costume. He's never been within ten feet of a camel and he's a big bore.'

She sighed. 'All right, who's interesting?'

'That little old lady over there,' he said promptly. 'The one in the orthopedic shoes.' A smile tugged at his mouth as he looked at her.

She was being reprimanded, she knew, ever so slightly, but he had a sense of humor, which was very reassuring.

'So what's interesting about her?'

'She knows how to ride a camel.'

Zoe laughed. She couldn't help it.

'She works for a relief organization in the Sudan,' he went on. 'She's on home leave.'

'You're kidding.' Zoe looked at the woman. She was tiny, wrinkled and gray and at least in her seventies—at first glance, just an old lady. On closer inspection, it was obvious that there was nothing old and doddering about her. She emanated a vivacious spirit, laughing and gesturing with her hands as she spoke.

'She seems rather busy now, but I'll have to go and speak to her later,' she said. 'By the way, I understand you've also worked in Venezuela. I have a friend who just moved there. Did you like it there?'

Behind the bright blue of his eyes, dark shadows moved. Or was she imagining it?

'Not particularly.' His voice had cooled considerably. 'Who told you?'

Not a good subject of conversation, obviously. Her heart fluttered nervously. 'Nobody. It was in Paul's file. He was born in Caracas, it said.'

He rubbed his temple with long, lean fingers, stroking at tension. Or pain. Or just out of habit. 'Yes, of course.'

'How's Paul doing?' she asked lightly. 'Did you talk to him?'

'Paul will be fine,' he said, a faint note of impatience in his voice. 'He'll see the light one of these days.' He took a drink from his glass, which held something amber-colored with ice cubes floating in it. Whiskey, probably.

The bunny bumped into him accidentally on purpose. 'Oh, I'm terribly sorry!' she exclaimed and beamed up at him with a toothpaste smile. 'Oh, I wanted to tell you that I found it *fascinating* what you said about the development politics in Argentina…was it Argentina?'

Zoe escaped with a sigh of relief. Saved by a rabbit, she thought, and gave a little chuckle. Well, she'd learned something about Mr Sinclair: not only did he not like talking about his son, he also didn't like talking about Venezuela. She wondered what had happened in Venezuela. She wondered what had happened to his wife.

She mingled, smiling, talking, listening, nibbling at exotic-looking little tidbits of food, trying not to be aware of Bryant, who, with amazing speed, had managed to get rid of the bunny once more and was mingling, too. She talked for quite some time with the little old lady, who was very interesting indeed, not to speak of sharp and full of humor.

'So, what did you think of her?' asked Bryant later.

'People like her give me great hope for the future,' she said. 'I hope I never dry up.'

'Do you worry about that a lot?'

She laughed. 'Actually, no.'

He put his empty glass on the tray of a passing waiter. 'And what are your hopes for the future?' he asked lightly.

'Oh, I have a catalogue full.' This was true enough, if not very specific. She wasn't ready to tell him her intimate dreams. She smiled. 'Mostly, I don't ever want to be bored. Or boring, for that matter,' she added.

'You are not boring,' he stated evenly, his blue eyes locking with hers.

She felt her heart leap a little. She mustered a bright smile. 'Thank you, that's a relief. I hope I can keep that up until old age.' She tucked a stray curl behind her ear. 'And what about your hopes for the future?'

'I've not given it much thought. May I get you another glass of wine?'

His personal future seemed to be another subject he did not care to discuss. It was getting to be quite a list.

'No, thank you, I've had enough.' She put her empty

glass on a nearby table, trying to find something safe to say. Fortunately, there was no need. Several people joined them and took over the conversation, which gave her the opportunity to listen and watch.

Watching Bryant's face and listening to his voice made her feel very much alive, a light, effervescent feeling that tingled all through her.

It was very late when she decided to leave. She felt good, very good. Her spirits had been much restored. Actually, she felt quite charged up. She smiled to herself as she skipped down the steps to the quiet, dark street. The air was crisp and cool and she took in a deep breath, lifting her face to the night sky. Stars, a swelling moon. Endless space full of mysteries. It made you think of magic and love and hope.

Life was exciting and full of promise.

She wished she could hug the feeling to her and keep it there always.

Paul's school performance did not improve in the following week. Twice in that time Zoe ran into Bryant as they were leaving for work at the same time. On both occasions her heart made a nervous little leap as she saw him—dressed in a business suit and smelling faintly of something clean and masculine. Neither time did he mention his son.

She'd seen him one other time, but he'd not seen her. The day after the party, Sunday, she'd taken a walk and noticed Bryant and Paul in the park, shooting hoops. Like Paul, Bryant had been wearing jeans and a T-shirt. He'd been like a different man, running, jumping, tossing the ball through the hoop with the smooth agility of an athlete. With her heart in her throat she'd watched his lean, muscled body twist and stretch and leap. Disturbing feelings had stormed through her—disturbing because of their intensity, because of the total lack of control she seemed to have over them.

It was frightening and exciting at the same time.

Sitting in her office, looking at the teachers' reports about Paul's work or lack thereof, she tried to concentrate on Paul and put Bryant out of her mind.

She called Paul into her office to have another talk with him. He sat huddled in a chair with his head down and stared at his hands as he fiddled with a paper clip. The body language was not promising. He answered all her questions with one of three mumbled answers: 'I don't know', 'I don't care' and 'It's stupid anyway'.

It was not the first time she had encountered a child like Paul with an attitude like his, yet she could feel her emotions getting the better of her. Bryant had to know something was wrong. Bryant had to take charge of this problem. Bryant had to care.

She wanted to do something, but scheduling another conference was most likely not going to work. She had to think of something else.

Something else—but what?

She needed inspiration, an idea, an opportunity. *Something*.

The next day she came home from school and found Paul outside sitting on the brick steps, his book bag next to him. He moved it to let her pass.

'Why are you sitting here?' she asked.

'I forgot my key.'

'Where's Mrs Garcia?'

He shrugged. 'She had to go to the doctor or something. My dad said I could be by myself today until he came home.'

'Well, I can let you into the front door. When is your dad coming home?'

He shrugged. 'I dunno.' He got up and followed her into the small hall they shared.

'Why don't you come up to my place and wait? You can have a snack and do your homework.'

He shook his head. 'Naw, I'm okay.' He sat down on the floor with his back to the wall.

She started up the stairs to her apartment. 'If you change your mind, just come on up, okay?'

'Okay.'

He did not come up. Half an hour later she went downstairs with a glass of apple juice and some cookies. 'I thought you might like something to eat.'

He put down the comic book he was reading and looked up in surprise. He took the glass and the small plate from her. 'Thanks.'

'You're welcome. When does your dad come home usually?'

He shrugged again. 'Different times.' He bit into one of the cookies. 'These are good,' he said.

'I made them myself. I'm famous for my chocolate-chip coconut cookies all over Africa.' This was rather an exaggeration, but it did get his attention.

'Really?' he asked. 'Did you live in Africa?'

She nodded. 'Several places. Last I was in Cameroon. I taught English at a boarding-school, and I was the girls' counselor too.'

His face closed up. 'Oh,' he said, and glanced back at his comic book.

Berating herself for her stupidity, Zoe went back up the stairs into her own apartment and left the door ajar, hoping to hear Bryant's arrival home. Paul was twelve, old enough to be on his own for a couple of hours when it was necessary.

It was five-thirty when she heard voices in the hall below. Bryant. Not so late.

Fifteen minutes later there was a knock on her door and Bryant stood in front of her, suit jacket gone, tie gone, shirt-sleeves rolled up. He handed her back the glass and small plate she'd given Paul earlier.

'Thank you,' he said, smiling. 'That was very nice of you.'

His hand was brown and strong, she noticed as she took the things from him. 'I asked him to come up here, but he refused,' she said, trying not to be affected by this tall, vibrantly sexy man standing in front of her. It was hopeless. Her heart fluttered crazily and her blood tingled.

'He told me.' His blue eyes held hers, as if looking for something. 'I'd like to take you to dinner tonight,' he said.

She laughed. 'Because I gave Paul some cookies?'

His mouth quirked. 'No, because I want to. Paul's going to spend the weekend with his cousin in Philadelphia. He'll be picked up in half an hour. I thought it would be a good opportunity to try out that little Thai restaurant on M Street and for us to get better acquainted.'

The gods are with me, she thought with sudden excitement. Maybe this was the opportunity she'd been looking for, an opportunity to find out more about what was going on. Maybe Bryant had changed his mind and decided he wanted to talk about Paul. Perhaps talking over dinner was easier than in her office, and in a casual atmosphere she had more chance to reach him.

'Do you like Thai food?' he asked.

She smiled. 'Oh, yes. I love fire and spice.' Oh, God, she thought, shut up.

A gleam in his eyes, a faint smile. 'Is that a yes?'

She tried to look sober, not to give him any ideas. 'Yes, it is,' she said evenly.

She stood in front of her closet finding something to wear. It was no use fooling herself—her concern for Paul was not the only reason she was interested in having dinner with Bryant. Bryant alone would have been incentive enough, but she was aware of very conflicting feelings. She was interested in this man, yet she was also wary.

She frowned. What to wear? There was not a whole lot of choice; since coming back home she'd had to buy a whole new wardrobe and most of her clothes now consisted of suits and dresses she wore to the office and casual sports wear. She took out a short, casual dress of multicolored silk with a wide belt. Fall colors—fiery orange, wine-red, glowing copper, golden yellow—colors that looked perfect with her chestnut hair and brown eyes, as the sales lady at Woodies had pointed out rather enthusiastically.

She put the dress on the bed and blow-dried her hair, thanking Mother Nature for her easy, manageable hair. It curled happily all by itself and she just let it do what it wanted to do. It hung just to her shoulders and often she put it up to keep it out of her face, but tonight she'd let it hang loose.

She slipped on the dress, put in gold hoop earrings and stepped into high-heeled shoes. Some carefully applied make-up, a dab of perfume and she was ready.

She picked up her purse and a soft knit jacket against the evening chill, and went down the stairs. Bryant came out of his door as she reached the hall. His glance moved over her discreetly and the look in his eyes left nothing to the imagination: he liked what he saw.

'I'm ready,' she said unnecessarily.

'Shall we walk?' he asked. 'It's not far.'

'It's nice out, sure.' She hoped her feet would manage in her high heels; they weren't used to such fashionable footwear.

It wasn't quite dark yet. It seemed strange to be walking side by side with this man, who was a stranger, and to feel this odd light-headedness at his presence. He wore camel trousers, a dark blazer and a shirt and tie, but even in the less formal clothes he looked impressive. He moved with an easy stride as if he enjoyed walking and was in no particular hurry.

Once at the restaurant they didn't talk about Paul. They talked about his work in Argentina and her work in Africa. Suddenly it was hard to think of Paul, of the things she'd wanted to say.

'Why did you come back to the States?' he asked, pushing his empty soup bowl aside.

'I woke up one morning and there was a message painted on my ceiling. It said, Go home! Be normal! Exclamation marks.'

He quirked a brow. 'Really?'

She grinned. 'Well, sort of. Maybe it wasn't actually on the ceiling. Maybe it was my imagination, or my subconscious giving me a message.'

He studied her face for a moment. 'So, you want to be normal?'

She put her spoon down. 'I thought I'd give it a try. It sounds so nice and comfortable.'

One corner of his mouth twitched upward. 'What made you go to Africa in the first place?'

She smiled. 'I was bored with nice and comfortable. I needed a challenge, an adventure.'

He nodded. Obviously it was a sentiment he could identify with.

'I started off in the Peace Corps,' she went on. 'It was quite an adventure, let me tell you, and one thing led to another and before I knew it I'd been gone six years. I'm twenty-nine. I thought it was time to come home and...settle down, work on my career here. Be normal.'

'Some people end up staying overseas forever,' he commented.

She twirled the stem of her wine glass. 'Yes. I have a friend who's been gone seventeen years, and I don't think he'll ever come back. I don't think he could ever adjust.'

'Are you finding it hard to adjust now?'

'In some ways, yes, very.' She grinned. 'Shopping is a major problem. All those choices! The decisions! But it's great being back. I love the fall, and the air is so clean and crisp, like drinking spring water. In Cameroon the air was so humid at times, you could ladle it up like soup.'

He looked into her eyes, saying nothing for a moment. 'You have beautiful eyes,' he said then. 'Warm and smiling. You must be a happy person.'

She laughed, taken aback a little. 'Oh, I think I am, most of the time.'

It was easy to talk to him. She was enjoying herself, and it seemed he was too. The food was delicious. The restaurant was small and very crowded, but she wasn't very much aware of the other people. All she was aware of was him—his voice and his thick blond hair swept back from a high forehead. A very noble forehead. She was aware of his blue eyes—eyes that made her quiver.

And she noticed his mouth, which was strong but sensual and caused disturbing thoughts in her head.

She liked the way he talked about his work, which involved the development of infrastructure in developing countries—bridges, dams, roads and airports. He was dedicated and committed, but not too enthusiastic about his state-side office job, which involved too much paper-pushing, discussing and negotiating, most of which annoyed and bored him. Obviously, he was a man of action, who needed to be involved in things happening—bridges being built, dams being constructed. She tried visualizing him in dusty khakis driving a Jeep. It was not difficult, even though all she had seen him in was impeccable, expensive city clothes. Not difficult at all, and she felt a secret twinge of excitement, which surprised her.

'You're looking forward to going overseas again, then?' she asked.

'When I find the right project, yes.'

'Don't you think it would be a good thing to settle down, for Paul's sake?' she asked. 'At least for a couple of years or so?'

His shoulders moved in a faint shrug. 'Paul's young. He'll learn to be flexible, to adapt.' He gave a half-smile. 'Important lessons to learn in life, don't you think?'

'Yes, yes, of course.' Here she was agreeing with him. 'Only,' she added, 'a lesson needs to be learned at the right time in the right place.' She hesitated for a moment. 'It's not going well with him in school, you know,' she said softly.

He met her eyes. 'I would prefer not to discuss Paul tonight. Would you mind?'

So that was not why he had invited her. One part of her rejoiced, another part was disappointed.

'I thought perhaps that's why you had asked me to dinner. To discuss Paul.'

'No. I asked you out for all the usual reasons.'

Her heart flipped in her chest. She took a drink of her wine. 'I see.'

'Is that acceptable?' he asked, amusement in his voice now.

She managed a smile. 'Of course,' she said lightly.

It was acceptable. It should be acceptable. It also complicated matters. Did she want to get involved with a man who didn't seem to take his son's troubles very seriously?

Maybe she was over-reacting. Maybe she was jumping to conclusions. After all, there were a lot of things she didn't know about them or their relationship at home. The image of the two of them in the park, shooting hoops, flashed through her mind. She'd heard Bryant's voice calling out praise and encouragement. She'd heard them laugh. Surely, their relationship seemed happy enough.

She gazed at her plate. The most important thing was to keep the channels of communication open. She took another bite of the spicy *nua pad prik*.

It was a little disconcerting how easy it was to forget about Paul when she was talking to Bryant, how easy it was to think other thoughts and feel other feelings, how easy it was not to think of Bryant as a father, but to see him simply as a man who was charming and interesting and who disturbed her heart-rate dangerously.

'Why did you become a school counselor?' he asked.

She laughed. 'I think it's the way I grew up. I have a super mother and all my friends used to love to come to my house and talk to her about their problems.' She took a drink of her wine. 'And I like kids. I don't think there's a deep, dark reason.'

She longed to know whatever he was willing to tell her about himself, but she found out little really personal information apart from the fact that he had grown up in the district where his parents still lived. His sister, married, now lived in Philadelphia and had two children, one a son Paul's age.

She told him she'd decided to try the city life after having grown up in the Maryland suburbs and that working at the Olympia International School had afforded her that opportunity. She told him she was an only child, that her father had died when she was seventeen and that her mother had remarried and now lived in Rome with her Italian businessman husband.

They walked home through the crisp evening air. The pungent scents of fall were all around. She was filled with an odd excitement. The streets were crowded with people—people walking home after eating at one of the many little neighborhood restaurants or seeing a movie, or people just taking an evening stroll with friends and mates. She liked the liveliness of the place, the many little shops—bookshops and spice shops and art shops and galleries and delicatessens.

He opened the front door and they stepped into the hall.

'Thank you very much for dinner. I enjoyed it!' she said, meaning it.

'I enjoyed it too.' His blue eyes looked into hers and it was suddenly hard to breathe. He leaned against the wall and observed her and she felt herself grow warm under his regard.

'I think,' he said slowly, 'something is going on between us.'

CHAPTER THREE

ZOE could not deny it. Something was going on between them—something elemental and instinctual that had nothing to do with reason or logic. Her heart was racing, her whole body tingled with anticipation.

'Yes,' she said huskily.

He pushed himself away from the wall. He stood very close. She stared at his chin, afraid to meet his gaze, afraid of what he might read in her eyes. This was crazy. She felt like a nervous teenager rather than the mature woman of twenty-nine she was. She knew what she wanted. She knew what he wanted. He was so close she could feel his body warmth, smell the clean scent of him, feel his breath brush across her cheek. With her heart throbbing, she raised her eyes to his.

Everything fell away—the small entryway with its faint smell of floor polish, her worries about Paul, time itself. His eyes mesmerized her, drawing her nearer.

She felt his arms surround her, saw his face bend towards her and then his mouth was on hers—warm and urgent.

Her whole being reacted to this kiss, wild tumult everywhere inside her as a storm of need swept over her. A soft moan escaped her and his kiss intensified. She kissed him back with a hungry passion that came from somewhere hidden deep inside her.

Finally, reluctantly, he released her mouth and with

his arms still around her he leaned back against the wall again, her body resting against the length of his, her face against the warmth of his neck. His breathing was ragged, as was her own, and Zoe closed her eyes, not moving, trying not to think. Thinking would spoil everything. She wanted to feel, only to feel.

Then, gently, he put her away from him and looked into her eyes. 'It's a good thing I'm not eighteen,' he said softly, a note of humor in his voice.

Her reason came back. And with it acute embarrassment. Sexual desire had its time and place and this had not been the time and place, surely. She hardly knew this man. It wasn't in her nature to lose control so totally, so quickly.

'I think I'd better go up,' she said with difficulty, wishing she could die on the spot. She had acted like a love-starved nymphomaniac. 'Thanks again for dinner.' She tried to be dignified as she walked up the steps, but her legs felt like rubber.

'Goodnight, Zoe.' His deep voice floated up behind her, intimate, knowing.

'Goodnight.'

Soon after, she lay in bed, unable to sleep. She thought of Bryant on the floor below, also in bed. At least, she assumed he was in bed. Was he thinking about her, wishing he had swept her straight into his apartment and taken her to bed and made passionate love with her?

She should not flatter herself. He was probably sitting on his sofa reading some report or other, contemplating the state of the infrastructure of some poor Third World country.

Then again, maybe he was taking a long, cold shower. She groaned into her pillow. What was the matter with her? Never in her life had she felt so totally bowled over by a man. It was terrifying. She wasn't sure how to handle it, what to do.

Well, one thing she did have to do: try to hold on to her sanity, not to let matters progress too fast so she'd lose control. A real relationship took time to develop and she wasn't in the market for something fast and fancy.

She pushed her face into the pillow. What she wanted was something solid and long-term. What she wanted more than anything was to find a soul mate, someone for the long haul. A man to build a life with, a man to be the father of her children.

Behind her closed eyelids was the image of a man with blonde hair and brilliant blue eyes.

She did not see or hear from Bryant in the next few days, which was a relief of sorts, even though she had expected it. He had told her during their dinner that there was a week-long international convention in town which meant he'd be busy till all hours.

Although she didn't get a glimpse of Bryant coming or going, what she did notice was a young blonde woman in the hall one afternoon with a grocery store paper bag clutched against her chest. She had a key and was trying to get into the Sinclair apartment.

'Hi!' she said cheerily, and gave Zoe a white-toothed smile. She was in her early twenties, Zoe guessed, and she had a fresh prettiness.

'Hi,' said Zoe, and started up the stairs, only to hear the sound of something dropping to the floor and a muffled curse. She glanced down. The girl had dropped the bag and the contents had fallen out.

Zoe went back down. 'Let me give you a hand.'

'Oh, thank you. That damned key. It wouldn't work.' She laughed. 'I'm such a klutz.'

She didn't look like a klutz. Her slim body looked sleek and sporty and well-coordinated. She wore slim-fitting jeans and a sweatshirt that read 'GEORGETOWN UNIVERSITY'.

Zoe put the stuff back into the bag—boxes of macaroni and cheese mix, a frozen pizza, a packet of hot dogs. The girl had managed to open the door and Zoe handed her the bag.

'Thanks a lot. Do you live upstairs?'

'Yes. I'm Zoe Langdon.'

'I'm Kristin Meyers. It's nice to meet you.' Her smile was bright. She radiated cheer and peppiness. 'See you!'

Zoe climbed the stairs to her own apartment wondering who Kristin was. Not that it was any of her business. Come to think of it, she hadn't noticed Mrs Garcia lately. Was she no longer working for the Sinclairs? Zoe stood in front of the window and looked down at the street, noticing Paul. His school bag hung by one strap from his shoulder. His head drooped and he focussed on his shoes as he kicked a pebble along the pavement. He'd been held after school today to do make-up work, work he had not done at home.

Maybe Kristin was a sitter, or a tutor, or a combination of the two. Then again maybe she was Bryant's woman of the week. 'Oh, stop it!' she said out loud to herself. It wasn't her business. She didn't care.

Yes, she did. Secretly, she kept waiting for Bryant to call or knock on her door, in spite of the blasted convention that made him come home late every night.

She turned away from the window. Something was happening to her and she didn't like it. She didn't want to feel this way. She didn't want his image in her head all the time. She didn't want to hear his words over and over in her mind.

'I think something is going on between us.'

She was not going to sit by the phone like a lovesick teenager and wait for Bryant to call her. He had kissed her very nicely—well, okay, *passionately*, she corrected herself—but that did not mean that he was now going to spend every night knocking on her door. He was busy and so was she—at least, she could make herself busy. She should do something about her social life, make friends.

She started a cooking spree and invited some of the teachers to dinner. She signed up for an evening class at the university. Maxie took her to a seminar on Indian spirituality on Friday night.

She wrote letters to her friends, called her mother in Italy, took long walks and read a big book, or tried to.

None of it helped one little bit. Her mind was determined to occupy itself with thoughts of Bryant, thoughts of him kissing her, touching her.

The trees had started to turn in vivid colors, the fiery orange and red of the maples joining the rich golden yellow of hickory and the warm, coppery brown of the oaks. In the morning the air was cool and clear and to Zoe it was like a gift of the gods. Walking to school she would drink in the air like champagne, feeling light on her feet and smiling at the world in general. Ah, fall was so glorious!

The six-weekly report cards came out, and Paul's was a miserable collection of failing grades. With a sigh of despair, Zoe sent a note home with Paul saying she wanted another conference with Bryant. He called her at home that night and just hearing his voice made her tingle all over.

'Hi,' she said. 'How was your convention?'

'Deadly. But it's over now. I received your note,' he went on, and there was a change in his voice, subtle but real. 'I have no time to come to school in the morning, and frankly I do not expect a conference to change anything.'

The lovely tingling stopped instantly and anger rushed through her in its stead.

'Have you seen his report card?'

'Yes.'

'Paul is in trouble, Bryant. You are his father. Don't you think you ought to do something?'

'I don't think a conference is going to accomplish anything.'

Not if he was not willing to cooperate, not if he didn't want help. 'So you're going to stand by and let him fail? Don't you understand that his behavior is a cry for help?'

'Listen,' he said impatiently, 'I'll come up and we can discuss it now if you like, but I can't do this on the phone with him in the next room.'

'Then come to my office tomorrow.'

'Your office, your apartment, what's the difference?' He sounded annoyed.

There was a big difference, but she didn't want to argue over time and place. In view of the situation, she was glad to have a chance to talk to him about Paul at all.

So she agreed, raced into the bedroom, looked at herself in the mirror and groaned at her faded jeans and sweatshirt. She put on some lipstick, brushed out her hair and a knock came on the door. He was dressed in jeans and a cotton sweater, and her heart leaped at the sight of him in his casual clothes. He looked sporty and strong and utterly male.

She told him to take a seat and busied herself pouring

them each a cup of coffee, her hands shaking. She sat down opposite him, willing herself to concentrate on Paul rather than Bryant.

She took a fortifying sip of her coffee. 'What did Paul say about his grades?'

He waved his hand casually. 'That this school is "stupid" and he wants to go back to his old school in Buenos Aires. I told him it was out of the question.'

She stirred her coffee. 'What did you say to Paul about his report card, specifically?'

'What do you think I said? I told him it was a disgrace and that I expected better from my son. I found him a tutor, but apparently that has not improved matters.'

Ah, Kristin. She couldn't help feeling a tiny sense of relief.

'The problem isn't that he needs help with his homework,' she said calmly. 'He knows how to do it; he just doesn't. He systematically refuses and that refusal is a symptom of the problem.' Her mind produced the picture of Paul slumped in his chair, head down, fiddling with a paper clip. 'Something is bothering him. He's not happy.'

He gave a crooked grin. 'He's twelve years old. Puberty's looming. Of course he's not happy. The world is a terrible place. Nobody understands him. Unfortunately, it's a phase he'll have to go through like the rest of humanity. It's growing-up time. He'll have to learn to adjust to changes and accept the inevitable.' He sighed. 'We can't go back to Argentina. There isn't a thing to be done about it.'

'Your move here was a big change and it's not easy to adjust to big changes like that,' she said.

He looked straight at her. 'Oh, I know,' he said slowly. 'Believe me, I know.' There was something odd about the way he said it, and deep down, way behind the brightness of his blue eyes, she saw a dark shadow.

Had any of this to do with his wife, Paul's mother? But she'd looked through all the records from Paul's school in Argentina and there'd been no mention of a mother—no name, no address, nothing.

'If you know,' she said gently, 'then you should be able to help him deal with it.'

He crossed his arms. 'I'm trying. We're having long father-son talks and I tell him it's important not to give in to these feelings, not to dwell on them, which is what he's doing. We eat huge bowls of ice-cream while I try to explain to him that what matters is the present and the future and that it takes courage to move forward without dwelling on the past.'

'It sounds easy, but it's a lot to ask of a boy of twelve. Maybe it would help if you acknowledged his feelings instead of telling him he shouldn't have them. He has the right to his feelings, you know. He's not miserable because it's so much fun.'

He stiffened. 'He is not miserable. I've been too busy lately, but the work is easing up and I'll be spending more time with him.'

She nodded. 'That's good.'

He came to his feet and stood in front of a water-color painting of an African market scene. After a moment he turned and glanced around. 'You have a nice place. Very personal, very cozy.'

'Thanks.' The tension had lessened, the atmosphere changed subtly. 'Can I get you a drink? I have Scotch, rum, dry sherry and white wine.'

'Scotch on the rocks, thanks.'

She went into the kitchen and he followed her in. When she took the Scotch bottle, he took it from her hand and set it on the counter. He put his hands on her shoulders and looked into her eyes and her heart began to thump.

'I wish you were just my upstairs neighbor,' he said, his mouth curving in an ironic smile.

'Yes,' she said. She did not avert her gaze. 'But I'm not.' She was his son's school counselor and she didn't like the way he dealt with his son.

'No, you're not. But could we for now pretend you are?'

Yes, said one part of her. No, said another. Pretending is dangerous.

She shook her head. 'I'm sorry,' she said with difficulty, 'I can't just pretend.' She slipped out from under his hands and took a glass from the cabinet.

'You're angry.'

'I'm frustrated.'

'Why? Why does Paul matter so much to you? There must be all kinds of kids with problems much more serious than his. Alcoholic parents, drug problems, whatever.'

True enough. She sighed, pushing the hair from her forehead. 'I'm frustrated because I know Paul is unhappy and I don't think your attitude is right.' She picked up the bottle of Scotch and poured out a measure into the glass.

'You don't think my attitude is right?' he repeated, a note of warning in his voice.

'Correct.' She looked straight into his eyes as she handed him the glass. 'You seem too casual about it. You don't seem to take it seriously.'

Silence. She felt a distinct chill in the air. He stood very still as he observed her.

'Are you saying,' he said slowly, 'that I don't care about my own son?'

Her heart pounded wildly. 'No, that's not what I'm saying. What I'm trying to say is that you give the impression of not taking his unhappiness seriously. You think all he has to do is be tough.'

'It's a tough life,' he said quietly, and there was nothing casual about his tone.

'So it is. And a little tender loving care and some understanding will help.'

He gave a humorless little laugh. 'You know it all, don't you, Counselor?' His voice mocked her. He tipped his glass back, finished the whisky in one go and with a forceful thump deposited the glass on the counter.

'Thank you.' He turned abruptly and marched out. She winced as she heard the door slam shut.

'Oh, damn,' she muttered. 'This is not good.'

Two days later she was cooking her dinner when there was a knock on her door. When she opened it she found Paul, looking nervous.

'You can say no,' he announced.

'Okay,' she answered, trying not to smile. 'No to what?'

'I gotta watch a show tonight on TV for a school project. It's about animals and the environment and conservation and stuff. I have to write about it for social studies, but I can't because Kristin broke our TV.' He took a deep breath. 'She's so stupid!'

'You can watch it here,' she offered promptly, relieving him of the difficult task of having to ask.

He gave a look of great relief. 'Thanks! It's at eight o'clock. I'll fix myself some dinner and then I'll come back at eight.'

'Isn't Kristin cooking you dinner?'

'She couldn't come today.'

'What about your dad? Isn't he coming home for dinner?'

'He'll be late. I'll leave a note saying I'm here.'

'So what are you cooking yourself for dinner?'

He shrugged. 'I'm just gonna have a sandwich.'

'I'm having chicken and rice. Chinese. You like Chinese?' Please, she prayed, let him like Chinese food. What we have here is an Opportunity.

His eyes lit up. 'Yeah.'

'How about having dinner with me and keeping me company?' she asked casually. She saw hesitation, eagerness, distrust flitting across his face. The eagerness won out.

'Really?'

'Why not? I'm by myself and I'm not that crazy about eating alone.'

'Okay.' He let out a sigh. 'I gotta leave a note for my dad and lock the door. I'll be right back.' He turned and rushed down the stairs with a speed that made her wince and fear broken bones or worse.

He was back in record time, carrying a notebook and pencil. This sudden interest in doing school work rather intrigued her, but she decided not to mention it. He was actually talking to her; she didn't want to spoil it now. She felt a rush of excitement. Maybe she could win his trust.

'Oh, cool, man!' he said as he walked into her living-room and glanced around. 'You got some weird stuff!'

'Go ahead and look,' she said, and went into the kitchen, where he joined her a little while later.

'That drum is awesome,' he said. 'Is it from Africa?'

She nodded as she stirred the chicken.

'Did you see a lot of wild animals?' he asked eagerly.

'In Tanzania I did.' She told him of her adventures in the Serengeti and he listened with awe. She smiled at him. 'Maybe there'll be some of that on that TV special tonight.'

'Yeah.' He watched her stir-fry the strips of chicken and vegetables. 'Kristin's cooking stinks,' he said contemptuously. 'All she ever fixes is hot dogs, macaroni and cheese from a box and pizza.'

It wasn't what she'd expected from a twelve-year-old. Kids loved that kind of food. 'You liked Mrs Garcia's cooking better?'

'Yeah. She still cooks for us most of the time. She comes in the morning now, you know, and Dad and I cook it or heat it up, whatever she says to do.' He shrugged. 'But when Dad's gonna be home late sometimes, then Kristin fixes something for me and her.'

'What kind of food do you like?' Zoe asked.

'Rice with stuff.' He frowned, thinking. 'And fish. Different things, you know?'

'Yes, I know.' She turned the burner off. 'All done. Let's eat.'

It was nice to see him eat with such appetite. 'I'm glad Kristin couldn't come today,' he said. He took another bite of his food. 'I hate her,' he said with his mouth full.

'That's too bad.'

He swallowed. 'She acts like she's my *mother*,' he said with contemptuous outrage.

'Maybe she likes you.'

His expression was a mixture of mockery and disgust. 'Hah! She likes my father, that's who she likes.'

'Must be tough,' Zoe said carefully.

'She's supposed to make me do my homework and

she's always correcting the way I talk.' He made a face. 'I was saying something about having left something in the car booth and she said, "In this country we call it trunk, not booth,"' he mimicked. 'And yesterday I told her Jeremy was giving me a lift to a birthday party and she said, "That's ride, Paul, not lift."' He did a fair imitation of Kristin's bright, cheery voice and Zoe bit her lip trying not to smile.

'I guess that annoys you,' she stated.

'Yes! And who cares, anyway? Kids at school talk in all kinds of ways. They're coming from all over the world and we understand each other pretty well most of the time.' He glanced at her and something dawned in his eyes, as if he just remembered something. 'Well, I guess you know,' he finished lamely.

It had just occurred to him that he'd been spouting off to the school counselor, the same person to whom he didn't want to divulge his feelings when called into her office at school.

But this was not the school office. This was her apartment and he was sitting here eating dinner with her. It was very clear to her that she'd make a big mistake if she mentioned anything related to school.

She offered ice-cream for dessert, which he consumed with gusto. Dinner over, he carried the dishes to the counter and stacked them in the dishwasher, which she found somewhat surprising.

'Thank you for dinner,' he said politely, looking at her with a smile. 'It was really good.'

She felt like hugging him, but knew better than to give in to the urge. There was something sweet and nice about this boy, something that tugged at her heartstrings. It was difficult to believe that this was the same boy who wouldn't open his mouth in her office.

'Are you going to watch the show too?' he asked, his tone indicating that he wouldn't mind if she did. So they watched together, and it fascinated her to see his reaction. Clearly he was deeply interested in animals, outraged by poaching and cruel slaughter. The program was nearly over when a knock came on her door. It was Bryant, and he did not look happy.

'Is Paul here?'

She nodded. 'He's watching a special program on TV. It's about over. Come on in.'

He shook his head. 'No, thanks. I apologize for my son,' he said curtly. 'He monopolized your evening.'

'I enjoyed having him,' she said. 'Don't worry about it.'

His face was tight. 'He shouldn't have bothered you. He has instructions to call his grandparents if something comes up. They gladly would have come and picked him up.'

Zoe shrugged. 'He came here and that was perfectly all right. We're neighbors.'

'He had no right to impose on you. I'll have a talk with him. It won't happen again.'

She stared at him, feeling anger rush to the surface with a force that was frightening. 'Don't you dare,' she heard herself say. 'Don't you *dare* tell him not to come here if he needs help!' She had no idea what made her say that, certainly not calm, rational professional thinking. She didn't care. Her heart was pounding and her hands were clenched into fists, as if she was ready to do physical battle.

He looked at her narrow-eyed. 'Are you telling me how to raise my son?' he asked slowly, and there was nothing nice and friendly in his voice, nothing sexy or appealing.

She looked straight into the cool blue eyes, her legs trembling. 'I'm telling you that Paul is welcome here any time, for whatever reason.' She refused to be intimidated by him. 'And if you have any common sense at all, you, as a single parent, should be grateful for that kind of offer.'

'And you're an expert on single parenthood too?' His voice was low and dangerous. 'Well, I don't need your advice, Ms Langdon.'

She was so enraged, she wanted to hit him. What was the matter with this man? Words failed her and it was just as well because Paul appeared next to her in the doorway. His eyes were bright and his face was alive.

'Hi, Dad! You got my note?'

'Yes, I did.' Bryant's face was suddenly calm again. 'Is the program finished?'

'Yeah. It was all about elephants and gorillas and crocodiles!' Paul's voice was full of enthusiasm.

Bryant studied his son's bright face, and Zoe saw no coldness now in his eyes, no anger.

'You liked it, I take it,' Bryant said, his mouth curving, softening the hard lines of his face.

'Yeah! It was really cool, Dad! You should've seen it!'

'I'm sorry I missed it.' He put a hand on Paul's shoulder. 'Let's go home and you can tell me all about it.'

'Yeah, okay!' Paul turned to Zoe. 'Thank you very much for having me over, Ms Langdon,' he said politely.

She smiled at him, suppressing the urge to ruffle his hair. 'Any time.'

He squeezed past his father and rushed down the stairs. Bryant followed him down, giving her a cool, polite goodnight.

'And you're an expert on single parenthood too?' His

words still hung in the air like a bad smell. It took an effort not to slam the door shut behind him. She gritted her teeth till her jaws ached.

The man was insufferable! She couldn't bear his arrogance.

The next day, soon after she had arrived home from school, a florist delivered a bouquet of white roses. She put them on the coffee-table, sat down and read the accompanying card.

'Your offer last night was generous and there's no excuse for my behavior. Please accept my apologies.'

She read it over several times, her mind awash with conflicting emotions. All day she had nursed her feelings of anger. Now what was she supposed to do?

The right thing. The polite thing. For the sake of peace. She looked at the roses. They were lovely. She remembered the dinner they'd shared, the way they'd kissed afterward, and warmth flooded her. And now this—this animosity between them because of Paul. A moan escaped her and she buried her face in her hands.

She had to do the polite thing and thank him for the flowers. After a solitary dinner that evening she went down the stairs and knocked on the door to his apartment. To her annoyance her heart was racing. She took a steadying breath, hearing footsteps approaching. The door opened and Bryant loomed over her. He wore a dress shirt but no tie, and his sleeves were rolled up.

'I came to thank you for the flowers,' she said, a little too fast. 'Apology accepted.'

His eyes met hers. 'Thank you.' He waved at the room. 'Please come in, have a cup of coffee.'

She hesitated, long enough for him to take her hand and draw her inside. He closed the door behind her, releasing her hand.

She raised a brow at him. 'You don't take no for an answer, do you?' she asked.

'You didn't say no,' he said smoothly.

Kristin sashayed into the room. 'Well, I'll be off, then.' She saw Zoe and stopped. 'Oh, hi!' she said, but there was a wariness in her eyes.

'Hi, Kristin,' Zoe said.

Bryant cocked an eyebrow. 'You've met?'

'Yes, at the door one day,' said Kristin. She wore a short black skirt and a red V-necked sweater without a shirt underneath. The V dipped enticingly between her breasts. 'Well, I'll see you tomorrow,' she said to Bryant, flashing him a bright smile. She opened the door. 'Goodnight.'

'How about a cup of coffee?' asked Bryant after she'd left.

'I'd love some.'

'Sit down; I'll be right back.'

She glanced around the living-room, curious and surprised. There wasn't much to see—some basic furniture, bare walls, some books and newspapers stacked against the wall. It was as impersonal and anonymous as a railroad station. No rugs on the floor, no plants, no artwork on the walls, nothing to indicate the character and personality of the people living there.

Bryant Sinclair was a well-traveled, sophisticated man, but the place did not reflect any of this. She had expected something very different—expensive furniture, wonderful artwork, beautiful rugs on the wooden floor— not this cold, bare place.

Then again, maybe it *was* representative of the person who lived here: functional, no frills, cold. She shivered, then remembered the night they'd had dinner, the conversation, his kiss. Bryant was not a cold man. Talking to him, she'd noticed caring and passion. And when he'd kissed her there had been fire...

She swallowed and focused on a stack of books on the table. Maybe his furniture and belongings hadn't arrived from Brazil yet. It could take months sometimes, especially if, for mysterious reasons, your stuff was sent to the wrong continent first.

He came back into the room, carrying a tray which he set down on the table. He handed her a cup. 'Here's sugar if you want it.' He took his own coffee and lowered himself into a chair across from her, leaned back and stretched out his legs.

Zoe spooned sugar in the cup and stirred it, glancing around the room meaningfully. 'Looks as if your stuff is still floating on the high seas somewhere,' she said lightly.

'It arrived a few weeks ago and I put it in storage. 'We're here only temporarily. This place belongs to a friend of mine and it was convenient for the short term.'

'Are you planning to leave soon?'

'I don't know when yet. It could be months, a year.' He frowned as he glanced around. 'I suppose I should do something, get some of the stuff out of storage.'

'Just a couple of rugs on the floor and some things on the wall would make a big difference,' she said casually.

'Dad?' Paul stood in the door. 'Oh, hi, Ms Langdon.' He glanced over at Bryant. 'Is Kristin gone?'

'Yes.'

'Good.'

'Paul!' said Bryant sharply.

'I hate her,' he said vehemently. 'You know I do!'

Bryant's face was taut with disapproval. 'You don't speak about people in that way.'

'Well, I don't like her! I want her gone!'

Bryant's face was full of dire warning. 'We'll discuss this later, Paul. This is not the time.'

Obviously, Paul knew when he'd reached the limits. Jaw clenched stubbornly, he turned and left the room.

'I'm sorry about that,' said Bryant. 'As you know, my attempt at solving the homework problem is not working out. But now let's talk about something else. For instance, do you like Lebanese food?'

She fought with herself. Should she pursue a personal relationship with this man when her professional relationship with him was a such a disaster? It was asking for trouble, wasn't it? She couldn't separate herself into two independent halves. That wasn't how it worked.

She clenched her hands. Every time the subject of Paul would come up, things would break down and tension take over. Yet if she decided to stay on a strictly professional footing from now on, she might never find out what the problem was. The more she got to know Bryant, the more chance there would be that she could help him and Paul.

Was she rationalizing? Was she just coming up with an excuse to go out with Bryant again?

She wanted to help. For a reason she did not understand she had special feelings for Bryant's son. She wanted to help Paul and chase away the sadness in his eyes.

'I love Lebanese food,' she said.

She did. She loved Lebanese food. She loved sitting with Bryant in the small, dark restaurant, listening to his voice, watching the expressions on his face.

The neighborhood was a treasure house of exotic little eating places and in the next few weeks they sampled Persian and Cambodian and Caribbean food. They talked about many things, but not about Paul's school experience. When they returned home, Bryant would kiss her senseless.

And that was where it stopped, as if by some unspoken agreement. He did not invite her to stay the night. She did not ask him to come up to her apartment. Something was holding her back. Did he sense she was afraid of the intensity of her own feelings? Or was he afraid of his own?

She was falling in love. She would lie in bed, aching for him, yet in the back of her mind, whenever she thought of him, there was that other face, hazy in the background. Paul. And whenever she thought of Paul warning bells rang, and a sense of helplessness would overwhelm her.

One afternoon Paul came to her apartment and asked if she would read his report about animal conservation.

'I thought you did that weeks ago,' she said, closing the door behind him.

'We had a month to do it. It's a big project. We had to make maps and use pictures and graphs and everything. I'm done now, but I kinda wanted you to read the written part. You know, to see what you think, and to fix my spelling.'

She frowned. 'Didn't Kristin come?'

His face grew tight. 'She's there, but I did my other homework. I told her I wanted to come here to…to ask you for help because you lived in Africa.' There was a gleam in his eyes. 'And she hasn't, so…anyway, she said I could.'

He had wanted to come to her, and he'd found a way. It almost made her smile.

'I'll read it right now. Can you stay?'

He nodded gratefully.

His report was an excellent piece of work, which wasn't a surprise. He'd been interested in the subject and he was a smart boy.

'It's very good, Paul.' She handed it back to him.

'Really? You think so?' He sounded so eager, it made her smile. Apparently her approval meant something to him. She felt a warm rush of excitement.

'Yes, really, but you knew that already, didn't you?'

He lowered his gaze and nodded. 'Yeah. I like animals. It was fun doing this report. My dad and I went to the zoo last Sunday. It was awesome.' He frowned. 'Only it's kind of sad to see those animals like that...I mean, not *free*.'

'Yes, I know what you mean, but it's good that people get a chance to see them.'

He nodded and glanced back at the paper in his hand. 'Did I make any spelling mistakes?'

'Just a couple. I marked them with pencil. I think your dad will be proud of this work.'

His eyes lit up. 'Yeah. I'd better go down. Thank you so much.'

Little by little, Paul was beginning to open up to her— a few words here, a couple of sentences there, as if he was testing her. This carefully rationed-out information, pieced together, became significant.

In Buenos Aires he'd had a best friend, an Argentinian boy nicknamed Kako. They'd played on the same soccer team, had shared the same interests in animals. Kako's parents had taken the two boys wilderness camping.

The day after she'd read his report he came up to her apartment again and showed her his pictures. There was an enthusiasm and vitality in him as he told her about the trip and the things he and Kako had seen. But when he closed the album he became quiet and sad.

'You must miss your friend,' she said, and saw the misery flicker in his eyes.

He shrugged casually. 'Yeah.' As if it weren't a big deal. But his eyes gave him away and she felt her heart flow over with pity.

'I had good friends in Africa, too. And I miss them a lot,' she said. 'It's hard when you move and you have to give up friends. It doesn't seem fair.'

He let out a sigh. 'Yeah.' There was a silence. 'But you've got to be tough,' he said then. 'You've got to adjust and make new friends.' The words sounded rehearsed and flat.

'Is that what your dad says?'

He nodded wordlessly.

'It's not always easy to make new friends.'

'No. 'Cos I still want to be friends with Kako. And his parents are real cool and everything and I loved being in his house, you know. It was like…like we were *brothers* more than friends. How can I just give him up? I mean—' He stopped and bit his lip and looked away, but not before she saw the gleam of tears in his eyes.

Her heart went out to him. He looked like a sad little boy for all his twelve years. Sad, and utterly lonely.

'What does your dad say when you tell him?'

He shrugged and looked down at his hands. 'He says I'll get over it. That I'll make new friends.' His voice was dull and his hands clenched tight in his lap. 'I don't wanna make new friends.'

'I understand how you feel,' she said. 'It makes you afraid you might lose them, too.'

He gave her a wide-eyed look, as if a new truth had hit him suddenly. He let out a deep sigh. 'Yeah,' he said.

Something had to be done. Paul was hurting and all his father was telling him was to be tough. She felt a sudden rush of determination. Bryant was going to have to see the light. He would have to start paying attention. It was obvious that he didn't like discussing Paul with her. He always avoided the subject. Guilt surged through her. And she had allowed him to. She had allowed him not to talk about Paul because it would invariably cause tension and she had wanted to avoid the tension as much as he.

She closed her eyes. She couldn't let it go on.

She was in love with Bryant the man. She was at war with Bryant the father. It was horrible to feel so torn, but her heart ached for Paul and he needed her help.

She called Bryant the next day and invited him to come up to her apartment for a drink. He arrived a little after eight, wearing a sweater over his shirt. He cradled her face between his hands and smiled down into her eyes. 'What an excellent idea,' he said, and kissed her. 'I was thinking about you today. I do that with a disconcerting frequency these days. I wonder what's wrong with me?'

Such magic words! She felt like melting into his embrace, but with a sense of new purpose she gently took his hands in hers and removed them from her face.

'I want to talk about Paul,' she said quietly, and felt him stiffen. 'I know we have studiously avoided talking about him because it always creates conflict. We've been deceiving ourselves if we were thinking this could go on.'

A shadow flickered behind the light in his eyes, a fleeting darkness washed away with his smile. 'Paul is my responsibility, Zoe. Please, let it be.'

She tensed. 'Paul is hurting. I can't just stand by and see him so unhappy. It's my job to help if I can.'

'Don't you think you're overstepping the boundaries of your professional duty?' he asked, and his voice had lost its warmth.

Her heart contracted painfully. 'I'm more than just a professional, Bryant! I'm a human being and I see what's going on and it makes me angry that you're so blind and unwilling, you can't see your son is hurting!'

'Oh, I know he's hurting. But giving in to it isn't going to help, is it?'

She was struck by the bitter anger in his voice and knew with sudden certainty that something else was going on behind the scenes. Things were never simple. The problems you noticed were usually merely the tip of the iceberg.

'Paul lost his best friend,' she said softly. 'A friend he says was like his brother, and all you tell him is to be tough and make new friends. It's not that simple, Bryant. His whole world was taken away from him when you moved here. He had nothing to say about it, no choice to make. That sort of thing makes people feel powerless and angry. That's a horrible feeling, Bryant.'

Something terrible flashed in his eyes. 'Is it?' he said softly—too softly. 'Thank you for your insight.'

'You're welcome. And here's a little more for you. If you think that demanding him to be tough is going to solve the problem, you're sadly mistaken. You can't ask him just to shove his feelings aside or deny them. If you don't allow him his feelings and acknowledge them, if you force him to suppress them, you're only fooling yourself in thinking they're just going to go away. They're not!'

'Spare me the psycho babble lecture, Zoe. I've heard it before.'

'But you aren't listening.'

A muscle jerked in his cheek. 'You've got it all figured out, haven't you—with your cozy apartment, your comfortable routine, your organized thoughts? You're so level-headed and full of common sense. You talk to the parents and you have all the answers, neatly tucked in your brain in drawers and file cabinets. Well, do me a favor, will you?' His voice was cold. 'Stay out of my relationship with my son! You may be the school counselor but you're not his mother! Find some other kid who truly needs your loving attention and let me handle my son myself! Now, if you'll excuse me?' He turned and slammed out of her apartment.

CHAPTER FOUR

PAUL'S face was flushed and he hung in the chair like a heap of misery as Zoe walked into the school's main office to do some photocopying.

She stopped in front of him. 'Paul?'

He gave her a glassy-eyed look and coughed. It was not a pretty sound.

'Are you sick?'

He nodded miserably.

Ann, the secretary, frowned at Zoe. 'We can't reach anybody. His father is not in his office, and there's no one at home at his grandparents' house.'

Paul coughed some more. It was clear he had caught a bad cold or a case of an early strain of flu. He did not belong in school. He needed a bed, a hot drink and some medication.

Zoe's thoughts raced, planning. 'I'll take him home,' she said. 'Call me if and when you reach his father.'

Having rearranged her schedule for the day, she bundled Paul in a taxi and found his house key in a side-pocket of his book bag where it kept company with some sticks of gum, a disgusting-looking plastic cockroach and assorted other junk. She decided that he'd be better off in his own bed than on the pull-out sofa in her apartment.

She had the taxi stop and wait at a nearby drugstore while she ran inside to get some cough and cold medicine, having no hope of finding anything in the Sinclairs' apartment, and having none at home herself.

Paul's bedroom was a complete contrast to the rest of the Sinclair apartment. Posters and pictures covered every square inch of the walls—Dracula with fangs dripping with blood, sports cars, music stars. No pictures of half-clothed female movie stars yet. It would not take long. Toys, books and a variety of clothes inhabited the shelves, dresser-top, floor and chair.

The bed had not been made, and she straightened the sheets and covers, then left the room so that he could put on his pajamas. She made him a hot toddy with tea, lemon and honey, which she got from her own kitchen upstairs.

'I'm sorry to bother you,' he muttered miserably as she gave him his medicine and the drink.

'I'm not bothered,' she said calmly, 'and besides, it's hardly your fault.'

'Are you gonna go back to school?'

'No, I'm staying here.'

'You don't have to. I'm just gonna go to sleep.'

'I brought some paperwork, so it's no problem.' She took the empty mug from him. 'Maybe you'll feel better when you wake up.'

'That was good,' he said.

'My mother always gave that to me when I had a cold. I don't know if it really helps, but it seems to.'

He nodded and glanced over at his messy dresser-top, his eyes focussing on something for a fraction of a moment; then he huddled under the covers, closing his eyes. An odd feeling, she wasn't sure what, made her survey the clutter on the dresser-top—books, socks, batteries, a model airplane, half finished. A photograph.

The air stuck in her throat. She stared at the picture—

at the beautiful woman smiling at her. A woman with long, straight black hair and gray eyes, holding a tiny baby in her arms. Zoe closed her eyes and swallowed with difficulty. Paul as a baby in the arms of his mother. That was what it had to be.

She drew in a steadying breath and quietly left the room, leaving the door ajar. In the living-room she stood in front of the window and looked unseeingly out into the street. All she could see was the face of the woman in the picture.

Paul's mother. Bryant's wife. Why had it shaken her so to see that photograph? Paul had a mother. Or had had. Bryant had had a wife. Rationally, she'd known that, of course, but seeing the picture had made it reality. There was a face now in her mind, a beautiful face with gray eyes and shiny black hair. The face of the woman Bryant had loved.

What had happened to her? Had she died? Were they divorced? Where was she now?

She took in a deep breath. It made no sense thinking about questions like that now; answers wouldn't drop out of the sky.

She turned away from the window. She'd been in this living-room several times over the past few weeks, and it did not look as bare now as it had the first time she'd been here. A beautiful Turkish rug warmed the floor and a few pieces of interesting artwork hung on the wall. It was still very much a man's place.

She made herself a cup of coffee in the kitchen, which necessitated checking out various cabinets and drawers in order to find what she needed. Well, it could not be helped. It was odd being alone in the Sinclair apartment and she felt vaguely uncomfortable. Maybe she wouldn't have felt that way had Bryant not been so furious with her last night. She closed her eyes and saw again his angry face, heard again his angry words.

'Stay out of my relationship with my son! You may be the school counselor but you're not his mother!' Well, here she was, taking care of his son, giving him medicine, putting him to bed, watching over him. 'Find some other kid who truly needs your loving attention and let me handle my son myself!' As it turned out, he wasn't here to take care of his son, so it was up to her to give him loving attention. She bit her lip and suppressed a smile. It was difficult not to see the humor of the situation. She wondered what he would say when he found her here in his apartment. Surely he would not suggest that she should not have done what she did? She settled herself on the sofa and went to work.

She was busy for the next two hours, then heard a key in the lock and her heart leapt. No one had called to say Bryant was on his way home.

But it wasn't Bryant. It was Kristin, carrying two textbooks.

They stared at each other, surprised.

'Oh,' said Kristin, 'I didn't know you were here.'

'Paul's sick. A bad cold, or the flu. The school couldn't reach his father, so I brought him home.'

'Is he in bed?'

'Yes. He's asleep.'

'I can't help him with his homework, then.'

'No.' But Kristin could stay with him until Bryant came home.

'I hate her,' Paul had said.

'What time is his father coming home?' Zoe asked.

'He said six or so.'

'I'll stay with him until he comes back,' she heard herself say. 'Go ahead and go.'

Kristin hesitated briefly. 'You think it'll be all right if I do?'

'I don't know why not.'

'Well, I really would appreciate it. I have a test tomorrow—biology—and I'd like to spend some time at the library.'

'I'll tell Bryant I told you to go.'

She smiled. 'Thanks.'

Zoe had expected her to move to the door and leave, but Kristin stayed put and bit her lip. 'Can I ask you a question?' she asked uncomfortably.

'Sure.'

'Is there something...I mean, are you and Bryant...?' She raised a hand. 'Sorry, it's none of my business. I shouldn't ask.' She turned and fled out the door.

Zoe stared motionless at the closed door. Kristin was in love with Bryant. It was no surprise, of course. Why shouldn't she be? She closed her eyes briefly. Oh, damn, she thought.

She looked in on Paul, who was still asleep. He seemed less feverish. It was an effort not to look again at the photo on the dresser, but she managed it.

She went up to her own apartment, took off her suit and quickly changed into jeans and a light cotton sweater. Paul awoke shortly after she returned.

'How do you feel?' she asked.

He began to cough again. 'Not so good,' he managed hoarsely. 'Can I have another one of those drinks?'

She fixed him another hot toddy, making herself a cup of tea at the same time. He asked where Kristin was and was visibly relieved when he heard she'd sent her away. 'I bet she'd make me do my homework whether I was sick or not,' he said. 'She's a witch.'

Zoe made no comment. Kristin seemed nice enough,

but she was probably under orders from Bryant to make Paul do what he was supposed to do, no matter what.

'My father was really mad last night,' Paul said uneasily. 'After he came back from your apartment.'

'I see,' she said carefully.

'He went to talk to you about my report card, didn't he?'

'Yes.'

'Well, it isn't your fault I have bad grades! He shouldn't be mad at you!' A coughing spell followed his angry words.

She smiled at his vehemence. 'Keep yourself calm, kiddo, and don't worry about me.'

He leaned his head back and closed his eyes. 'It isn't fair,' he muttered. 'Nothing is fair. My life stinks.'

Zoe decided not to react to his statement of discontent. She allowed him to move to the sofa in the living-room and watch television, but an hour later his fever was up again and he crawled back into bed after she'd given him another dose of medicine. He didn't want the chicken soup she offered.

At ten to six she heard the front door of the building open and close. Voices, laughter in the hall. A female voice. Then a key in the apartment door. A tall, smiling woman came into the room, followed by a grinning Bryant.

Zoe's heart turned over in her chest. Bryant's grin faded as he saw her on the sofa and his brows rose in surprise.

'Paul is sick,' she said. 'They couldn't reach you or his grandparents, so I brought him home.' She got up and gathered her papers.

'What's wrong?' Bryant's voice rang with instant alarm.

'A bad cold, or the flu. He's been running a fever and he's been coughing. He's in bed. I gave him a dose of medicine at five. He can have another one at nine.'

Bryant strode out of the room without another word, leaving her alone with the woman, who smiled at her and held out her hand. 'I'm Kate Carrington. I'm afraid it's my fault he wasn't in his office. He was at Dulles airport picking me up and the plane was a little late, and then there was a car accident and we were held up for almost an hour.'

Zoe shook her hand and introduced herself. 'It doesn't matter. I was glad to help. I live upstairs, so it's no problem.' She picked up her papers. 'I'm off. Nice meeting you.' She smiled politely, opened the door and closed it again. Expensive luggage stood in the hallway. She rushed up the stairs and into her own apartment, dumped her stuff on the coffee-table and sagged down on the couch. She closed her eyes and took a deep breath.

Her heart was pounding. From running up the stairs. From seeing Bryant. From seeing Bryant come home with a beautiful woman.

He was free to come home with ten beautiful women. Her reaction was ridiculous. She could be his sister, his cousin...

The phone rang.

'Why did you run off so fast?' asked Bryant.

Run off? She gritted her teeth. 'You were home; I didn't need to stay.' She forced her voice to sound calm.

'I appreciate your taking care of Paul,' he said.

She allowed a short, significant silence. 'You're welcome,' she said then, her voice polite. I hope I didn't overstep the boundaries of my professional duties, she was tempted to add, but managed to keep the thought to herself. The last thing she wanted was to be childish and petty.

'I'm ordering some Japanese food. I'd like it if you'd join us.'

Did he think she was crazy?

'Thanks, but I can't. I have a class tonight.' Which was even true.

She felt miserable, and angry because she did. First there'd been the picture of his wife, then Kristin giving away that she'd fallen for Bryant, and topping it all off was Bryant himself coming home with a gorgeous female. There were some messages here, if she wanted to see them. Or omens.

After a quick dinner, she left early for her class. Afterward she joined a group of fellow students and went out for a drink in a jazz bar. She didn't feel like going home, walking in the front door, wondering what was going on behind Bryant's door. It was late when a taxi dropped her off. The suitcases were gone from the entryway. Moved inside? She gritted her teeth as she walked up the stairs. She couldn't remember ever feeling this way—jealous, miserable, angry.

She couldn't remember ever feeling about a man the way she felt about Bryant.

He knocked on her door two days later. 'I'm sorry it's so late, but I saw the light on in your living-room when I came home,' he said.

'How's Paul doing?' she asked, trying not to feel the powerful tug at her heart as she looked at him.

'Better, a little. He's been at my parents' house. My mother is clucking over him.' He arched a brow. 'May I come in or is it too late?'

She stepped aside and he entered the room. 'I was just

balancing my check-book. It's twenty-three cents off and I can't find it.' She rubbed her head. It was aching.

'Make an adjustment and be rid of it.'

She flopped down on the sofa. 'It bugs me.'

He gave a lopsided smile. 'Are you a perfectionist?'

'No, just stubborn.'

His eyes met hers. 'I see.'

She knew what he saw. Her gaze did not waver as she looked back into his eyes, saying nothing.

'Could be dangerous,' he said softly.

'Could be dangerous not to be,' she returned flatly, tucking her legs under yogi style.

He nodded, pushing back his jacket and putting his hands in his pockets. 'So where do we go from here?' he asked.

'What did you have in mind?' She did not sound friendly. She had not forgotten the way he had spoken to her the night before Paul had become ill.

'I was asking you,' he said.

She studied his tie for a silent moment. 'Contrary to what you believe,' she said, 'I don't have an answer or a solution for everything. I don't know where we go from here.' She met his eyes. 'I can't pretend not to be concerned about Paul.'

And there were other things she couldn't pretend. Images of faces floated before her mind's eye—his wife's, Kristin's, the face of the woman he'd brought home.

She did not feel up to thinking about it. It was late. She was tired. She wanted him to leave.

'I appreciate your concern, but—'

'But you wish I'd mind my own business,' she finished for him. She massaged her temples. 'I don't want to talk about it right now. I will promise you that I'll check all those neat drawers and file cabinets in my neat little brain to see if I can come up with a solution, but right now I want to go to bed. I'm tired and I have a headache.' And I want you to leave, she added silently.

'We'll talk another time.' Businesslike, determined. In one stride he stood before her and reached for her hands. He drew her carefully to her feet straight into his arms and kissed her hard. I want you, his kiss said. Don't think I'll let you go.

A breathless moment later he closed the door quietly behind him, leaving her with her head spinning.

The next morning she awoke not feeling very well and by the time the school day was over her head ached and her throat felt raw. She was getting it too. In the last few days several other students had been reported sick as well.

At home she swallowed some aspirin, which helped a little, but by the time it was eight that night it was obvious that she'd caught the virus like the rest of them.

She should have bought some cold medicine on her way home, but her mind had been too occupied with getting there. Perhaps Bryant still had the stuff she'd been feeding Paul. She would have preferred not to have to call him, but she had no choice.

'It's gone,' he informed her, 'but I'll get you some.'

She was too miserable to object. She unlocked her door and crawled back on to the sofa, looking glassy-eyed at the television screen where bikinied girls frolicked on a palm-fringed beach. They were slim, tanned and supremely healthy and made her feel even worse.

Half an hour later Bryant knocked on the door and she called out for him to come in, her voice raw and raspy.

He carried a paper bag in one hand, a half-full bottle

of Scotch in the other. In his jeans and sweatshirt he looked the picture of virile male health. She felt like an old rag, but was beyond caring.

He perused her face, making no comment. He probably thought she looked like hell, but was too much a gentleman to say so.

'Have you taken your temperature?' he asked.

'No. I have a fever for sure, but I'm not delirious. Dying, but not delirious.'

He lifted up the bottle of Scotch. 'Maybe a whisky toddy will revive you.'

'What's in the bag?'

'Medicine, lemons, honey, chicken soup, chocolate truffles. Everything you need to get you back on your feet.' He disappeared into the kitchen.

Chocolate truffles. Good grief. She would have laughed had she not felt so rotten.

A few minutes later he handed her a hot whisky toddy and a dose of medicine.

'Thank you.' She took a gulp of the hot drink. He'd been liberal with the Scotch, but it tasted good.

'Don't drink it so fast,' he warned.

'Don't you tell me what to do,' she said crankily. 'It's good and I need all the help I can get.'

'What else would you like?'

'I want to go to bed and die.' She finished the drink. 'But first I'd like another one of these.' She handed him the glass mug.

'I think one of them is enough. How about some orange juice?'

She gritted her teeth. She felt hot and feverish and had no patience for his paternalistic attitude. 'I want a toddy. With whisky. And don't you tell me what I can have or not!' She glared at him, but her eyes burned and she closed them and sighed.

'Are you sure?'

'Of course I'm sure!'

He made her another toddy. It was hot and sweet but not as strong as the first one. He'd made himself a Scotch on the rocks and they watched TV while they had their drinks. She was glowing all over.

'I feel much better,' she said, putting down the empty mug. It was a lie. She felt positively horrible. Her head was spinning.

He stretched his legs and leaned back in his chair as if he had no plans to leave. 'Good. Paul did say your toddies worked miracles. Did you put whisky in his?'

'Are you crazy? I'm a law-abiding citizen. You could have had me arrested. Then they'd have thrown me in gaol and I'd have been out of your way.' She glowered at him. 'Lucky you,' she added. She didn't know what made her say that except that she seemed to have no control over her tongue. She felt wretched. She wanted to cry. She wanted him to leave. No, she didn't. She wanted him to put his arms around her and hold her tight. If only he would hold her she would feel so much better.

His eyes held hers for a moment. 'I don't want you out of my way.'

She pushed her damp hair away from her forehead. 'That's not the impression you gave me a few nights ago. You were furious and you said terrible things to me.'

He crossed his arms. 'You want to argue about it?'

'Yes,' she said. 'I want to tell you you are a stupid, selfish swine. All I want to do is help Paul.' She began to cough. Tears ran down her cheeks. A wave of misery washed over her. A jumbled collage of sounds and sights tumbled in her mind—voices, faces.

'Did you know Kristin has a thing for you?'

He cocked a brow, but said nothing.

'And who the hell was that woman you brought home that night?'

A small smile tugged at the corners of his mouth. 'Ah, jealous, are we?'

'No! I'm just sensible. I don't want anything to do with you if you sleep around.' She began to cough.

He handed her a box of tissues. 'I see.'

'I know how to take care of myself.'

'Of course,' he said soothingly.

'And don't you laugh at me!'

'I'm not laughing at you. I wouldn't dare laugh at a smart and intelligent woman.'

She wiped at the tears running down her cheeks. 'I'm not so sure you are smart.'

'Because I invited a woman into my apartment?'

'Did you sleep with her?'

'You're being very indiscreet. I invited you into my place and I didn't sleep with you.'

'I don't sleep around.'

'That's a big relief because neither do I. Kate is a friend. She and her husband live in Buenos Aires and they're friends of mine. She went to a hotel for the night. Satisfied?'

He looked down at her with his hands in his pockets, looking disgustingly self-confident. He was big and strong and overpowering. She didn't know if she loved him or hated him. She wanted to go to bed and sink into the blessed oblivion of sleep.

'I'm going to bed.'

'A splendid idea. Come along and let me help you.'

'I can get there myself.' She stood up but her legs were shaking. He put an arm around her to steady her and led her into her bedroom without another word. She did not have the strength to object. He helped her take off her robe and draped it over a chair.

'A flannel nightgown,' he commented. 'You look positively ravishing.'

'Oh, shut up and leave me alone.' She crawled into bed and pulled the covers up to her chin.

'I don't like flannel nightgowns. They don't do a thing for me.'

'So who cares?' She closed her eyes.

'I thought you did. I thought you wanted to sleep with me.'

'You're hallucinating. Your ego is out of control.'

'You're high on Scotch, sweetheart. You should hear yourself talk.'

Another coughing spell overtook her. Tears ran down her cheeks again. 'Oh, go away!' she said at last. 'Please let me suffer in peace!'

He grinned. 'You are a lousy patient, you know that?'

'You're making me mad! What kind of bedside manner is that?'

'Okay, okay. I'm leaving. I'll come and check up on you in the morning.'

'Don't bother.'

He bothered. He was back at seven, letting himself in with a key he'd apparently taken out of the lock the night before. She'd not thought of putting the chain on the door, so he'd been able to walk right in. He stood in the doorway of her bedroom, dressed to kill in a suit and tie, ready to conquer the world.

She'd had a miserable night and she was not feeling

better. Seeing him standing there in all his male splendor did nothing to help matters. She'd seen the demoralizing spectacle of her appearance in the bathroom mirror only minutes before. Her hair was limp and damp, her face puffy, her nose red, her eyes bleary. And her flannel nightgown was a mass of wrinkles.

'You're awake,' he stated. 'Feeling any better?'

'No.'

'I'll make you some tea and toast.'

I don't want tea and toast, she was tempted to say, annoyed by his take-charge attitude. Couldn't he just ask if she wanted tea and toast?

The hot tea did her good, but all she could manage was a couple of bites of toast. He sat by her bed while she ate, as if he had all the time in the world, which she was sure he had not.

'I'm all right,' she said. 'Thanks. Go ahead and go to work. And thank you for being here last night. I know I'm a terrible patient. I hate being sick and I get very cranky.'

'Yes, I noticed.' His mouth curved in amusement. 'Cranky, not to mention loose-tongued.'

She closed her eyes and groaned. She remembered. She wasn't so far gone that she didn't remember the things she had said and asked.

'It was very enlightening,' he commented.

'Don't embarrass me.'

'I'll go to work.' He fished a business card from his pocket. 'I'll be in my office all day. Call me if you need anything. I'm at your service.'

She stared at the card. It was very impressive. Not the card of a person who'd come running to tend to someone with the flu.

'Thank you.'

He bent down and kissed her forehead. 'I'll see you later.'

It was that quick kiss that almost made her cry after he left. He was being perfectly nice, as he'd been last night, and she had been a miserable witch.

The day yawned in front of her. She wasn't sleepy, but she didn't feel like reading. She called her mother in Rome, but no one answered. She wished someone would drop by, as people had done all the time in Africa. Her house there had been so different, the furniture old and shabby, government issue. Yet even there she had managed to make it a cozy place. People had gathered at her place for dinner, or coffee, for conversation and good times. She needed people around her. There was no one here. It was depressing.

She watched TV, leafed through some magazines, had a glass of orange juice and some crackers and went back to bed.

She awoke in the middle of the afternoon, feeling a little better. She had a shower, put on a clean night-gown—pink flannel—and settled on the couch with a cup of herbal tea and honey and dialed Rome. No one answered at her mother's house. She sat with the phone in her hand feeling lonely and sorry for herself.

Bryant walked in just after four, carrying a big, extravagant bouquet of flowers. She was so glad to see him, she almost cried. Instead she sneezed and had a fit of coughing.

'Hello to you too,' said Bryant in answer. 'Not doing so well, I see.'

'I'll live.' She blew her nose. 'You're going to catch it too. You shouldn't be here.'

'Yes, I should. I'm immune.'

Of course he was. No mere flu virus would dare attack

that splendid male body. It'd take one look at those blue
eyes and steel muscles and flee in the other direction.

'The flowers are beautiful,' she said. 'I think they'll
go well in that big white pitcher on top of the refrigerator. Would you mind?'

A few minutes later the flowers decorated the coffee
table. It was a very cheerful sight. 'Thank you,' she said.
She glanced at the clock. 'You're very early.'

'So I am. Would you care for some home-made
chicken soup?'

She stared at him. 'Home-made? You made chicken
soup?'

'No. My mother sent it over for you.'

'I don't know your mother.'

'She knows you. Paul told her about you.'

'I see. And she made me chicken soup.'

He gave a crooked grin. 'I expect the cook made it,
but no matter.'

The cook. Of course. How silly of her.

'I'd love some soup,' she said. 'That was very nice
of your mother.'

'My mother is a very nice person. Annoying, infuri-
ating, interfering, but very nice.' He opened the door.
'I'll be back in a few minutes.'

It took her several days to recuperate, but Bryant's at-
tentions helped. He was perfectly nice, perfectly consid-
erate and friendly. She grimaced at herself. Which was
not something she could say of herself. She had no patience with herself when she was sick, nor with anyone
around her. It seemed as if some other person inhabited
her miserable body—a very unreasonable, irrational, insufferable individual.

She went back to work on Friday, feeling a bit weak

in the legs yet, but determined to be done with being
sick, done with being an insufferable person. When she
came home that afternoon, she was happy to see a letter
from Nick. It consisted of several pages with colorful
illustrations, including a huge crooked heart.

She began to read, smiling. All the usual news and
gossip about the school and the town were described in
vivid detail, followed by his informing her that he'd had
an enlightening dream. About her. About them. She was
his best friend, he said. He still missed her painfully.

I have come to a momentous understanding. I never
realized how much you meant to me until you were
gone. The emptiness in my life is having a very puri-
fying effect on my brain. Sometimes I see things quite
clearly now, as opposed to the rather muddy way I
think normally. Yesterday, in a flash of lucid thinking,
this occurred to me: Perhaps we belong together, Zoe.
You and I! Together! A tantalizing thought!
    We get along so well. We understand each other.

Zoe lowered the letter in her lap. It was the truth. They
did get along well and they did understand each other.
He was a true friend. He made her laugh. He had always
been ready to help. She had missed him, too.

I think you should come back here. We'll get married
and be done with all this loneliness business—you
being lonely, I being lonely. What for? Why not be
together? So start packing. And while you're at it do
me a favor and bring me a couple of packs of boxer
shorts, size medium. Something bright and colorful
would be good.
    I suggest a tribal ceremony. So much more dra-

matic, don't you think? I suggest we go on a honeymoon in Zimbabwe and go camping in the game parks. Camping is the only way to go, but don't you fear—I will protect you—see illustration—and we will have a wonderful time in Eden.

She laughed as she examined the drawing which depicted a night scene with a tent encircled by roaring lions. Inside, the two of them huddled in a ratty double sleeping-bag, she looking terrified and clutching him around the neck, he looking fierce and clutching a bow and arrow. Nick was an artist. He sure knew how to draw.

She continued reading the letter, which went on about the adventures the two of them would have traveling the world. It ended with a theatrical plea for her to return to Africa, straight into his lonely, waiting arms. A crooked red heart filled up the rest of the page. 'I LOVE YOU!' he'd scrawled across it. Grinning, she put the letter down on a side-table to reread later. Nick's letters were worthy of at least a couple of readings, and this one certainly was a masterpiece.

It had been her first day back at work, and she could tell that having been ill had taken its toll. By eight that evening she was feeling distinctly droopy and decided to make an early night of it—have a leisurely bath, watch some TV and sleep as long as she wanted to. It certainly was no night to go out; it had started to rain and a fierce wind was blowing and making threatening noises around the outside of the house and in the trees. Inside it was warm and snug and staying home was no punishment.

She lay in the bath with fragrant bubbles up to her chin, thinking about Nick's letter. 'We'll get married and be done with this loneliness business'.

Going back to Africa certainly had its appeal. Or South America, or Asia, for that matter. She could not deny that at times she felt just the tiniest bit restless. And somewhere, deep down, she felt a spark of doubt about having done the right thing in coming back.

'Oh, grow up,' she muttered to herself. 'You made a conscious choice to come back. Now make it work.'

She had everything she wanted, didn't she? A good job, a lovely apartment—quite a nest actually. She was beginning to make friends.

The phone began to ring. She let it go, having no desire to climb out of the water to answer it and drip water all over her lovely wooden floor. If it was important the person would call back.

She was hardly out of the bath a little while later when someone was knocking on her door. It had to be Paul, or Bryant. The street door had been locked and no one had rung the bell. She tightened the belt of her robe and wrapped a towel around her wet hair.

'Who is it?' she asked before taking the chain off the door.

'Bryant,' came the curt reply. She opened the door.

His face was ashen and her heart leaped into her throat.

'What's wrong?' she asked.

'Paul's gone.'

'*Gone*?'

'He left a note saying he was running away and wasn't coming back.'

CHAPTER FIVE

ZOE swallowed hard. 'Come on in,' she managed, closing the door behind him as he entered. 'Maybe he just went to somebody's house and he's fine.' She uttered the words automatically, trying to douse the fear that ran like brushfire through her.

Deep lines were edged by the side of his mouth. 'My mother was supposed to pick him up at school, but he called her and said he was going home because you were better and he wanted to work on a school project with you.'

'He wasn't here.' Her throat felt dry. 'I didn't see him.'

'He did come home because he packed some of his things and left the note for me to find when I came home tonight.' He rubbed his face. 'I called everyone I could think of. Nobody knows anything. What the hell does he think he's pulling? Where does he think he's going to sleep?' His voice was rough with frustration and anger, his eyes were dark with worry.

Rain slashed against the window-panes and the thought of Paul being out in the wet and stormy night made her shiver involuntarily. 'Did you call the police?'

He gave a bitter little laugh. 'Do you know how many teenaged runaways there are every year? They said he'll most likely turn up on his own tonight, but they'll keep an eye out for him. If he doesn't show up by tomorrow,

I should call again.' He fished a sheet of paper from his pocket. 'These are the kids from his basketball team. Can you think of any other kids he knows?'

She glanced down at the names and numbers, racking her brain about other names he might have mentioned, or boys she'd seen him with. She shook her head. 'I'm sorry, no.'

His face worked. 'Dammit,' he said, the paper crumpling in his hand as he clenched it. She wished there were something she could do, that she had some useful advice to give, but there was nothing. How could Paul have done such a thing? Where could he have gone? She heard the wind in the trees outside. It was a terrible night out there—surely he wasn't roaming the streets of the city? Surely he hadn't done something stupid? Her heart twisted with anxiety.

The phone rang and she noticed Bryant start and reach for it, then drew back. 'Sorry,' he said. 'I had my calls routed through here before I came up; I didn't want to miss any. I knew you were home but you didn't answer the phone when it rang.'

'I was in the bath-tub. It's fine.' She felt the towel slipping from her head and she held it in place with one hand while the other picked up the receiver. A salesperson trying to sell her car insurance. She got off the phone fast.

Excusing herself, she went into the bathroom, took the towel from around her head and brushed out her wet hair. There was no make-up on her face and she still looked pale, but her appearance was not a big concern at the moment. She went into the kitchen and made two cups of coffee.

'Here,' she said, putting the cups on the table. 'Sit down.'

He didn't even hear her. He prowled restlessly through the small room, then stopped and stood in front of the window and stared outside. She looked at his back, seeing the tension in the taut muscles, and feeling something twist inside her.

'What happened? Why did he run away?' she asked.

'I'm sure you can imagine,' he said sharply, not turning to face her. 'You of all people ought to know.'

Stay calm, she told herself. She took in a careful breath.

'What specifically happened that made him want to leave? What did you say to him?'

He shoved his hands in his pockets. 'I gave him my standard speech. That it was time for him to grow up and accept the fact that people leave and move on. That it was useless crying over the inevitable. That he had to have courage and focus on his life here and now and do the best he could to make it good.' He spoke to the window, his back still turned to her. 'Life is tough,' he went on. 'Crying doesn't help. He's got to learn to be tough.' It sounded as if he'd said it a hundred times. He probably had.

Zoe was silent and the words hung in the air. They were all the things she'd been telling herself at one time or another, but there was a big difference. Whenever she'd had problems, there'd always been her mother or a sympathetic friend—someone who understood her anger or grief, someone who said it was all right to cry. At least for a while. Paul had to do it alone. Paul was not allowed to cry.

Bryant turned to face her, his mouth curving bitterly. 'You've been telling me I've been handling my son wrong. Well, I guess you were right. Does that give you any satisfaction, Miss Counselor?'

She stared back at him, feeling anger rise to her head in a wave of heat. 'Of course, I'm delighted!' she said caustically. 'I'm overjoyed! This is just wonderful! Paul is hanging out God knows where and I'm supposed to be happy because it proves I was right! What's the matter with you?'

Well, she knew what was the matter with him. He was worried and angry and feeling guilty and probably not in full command of all his sensibilities. He felt attacked and was lashing out in defense.

He massaged his neck. 'I'm sorry,' he said roughly. 'I didn't know what I was saying. I didn't mean to take my anger out on you.'

Anger. That was what he called it. Anger was manly. Worry, fear, pain and guilt were not. She almost smiled. 'I know,' she said. She picked up her coffee and took a gulp.

He made for the door. 'Sorry to bother you.'

'Oh, for heaven's sake, sit down! Have your coffee. What do you think I'll do if you leave? Go out dancing?'

He met her eyes and the silence seemed heavy with meaning. 'You really care about Paul, don't you?' His voice had dropped a notch.

Her hand shook suddenly. She put the cup down. 'That's not so hard to do, you know.' Her voice quavered and she kept looking down so that he couldn't see her face, couldn't see the tears that suddenly swam in her eyes.

'I know,' he said huskily. 'Oh, dammit, Zoe!' He sat down next to her and put his arms around her.

She put her face against his shoulder and took in a slow, deep breath, trying not to cry. 'He'll be back,' she said. 'He's too smart to do something stupid.'

'He already did something stupid.'

'But he'll realize it and change his mind.'

He was silent. They sat there for what seemed like a long time. Then he jumped up and dragged his hands through his hair. 'I've got to do something. I can't just sit here and do nothing.' He strode to the door.

'Where are you going?'

'I don't know. Look for him.' He opened the door. 'Please, stay by the phone.'

'Life is tough. Crying doesn't help. He's got to learn to be tough.'

It was more than just advice. Something else was hidden in those words. Bryant was telling his son to be tough because he himself had had to be tough. An image flashed through her mind—the picture of the woman holding the baby in her arms. Paul's mother. Bryant's wife.

'Accept the fact that people leave and move on'.

Had his wife died? Had she left?

He'd never talked about his wife, and she hadn't asked, hadn't *wanted* to ask, for whatever reason. Her stomach churned. There was too much she didn't know, too much she didn't understand. Too much she'd tried not to think about.

She pressed her hands against her closed eyes until she saw stars.

And now Paul was gone.

Three hours later Bryant came back, drenched and muddy, and looking dreadful. She'd been going crazy with worry. She'd called all Paul's teachers, hoping someone might have heard something or was aware of something. Thank God for modern technology. She could use the phone and hear a beep if someone else was trying to reach her on her line. Otherwise she might not have dared using the phone, afraid that she might miss a call from Paul.

Calling the teachers had at least given her something to do, even though she'd had no great hopes that she would learn anything useful—and she hadn't.

'You didn't find him,' she said, stating the obvious.

He ran his hand through his dripping hair. 'No. Any phone calls?' His voice was dull. He knew the answer already.

'No, I'm sorry.' She gave him a hand-towel. 'Where did you go?'

He wiped his face and hair. 'I drove around the neighborhood. I checked the library. I walked around the park, all around the school.' He balled the towel and flung it to the floor. 'Dammit, he's got to be somewhere!' His voice held rage, worry and helplessness. He was not a man who took well to feeling helpless, she could tell. The terrible thing was that she felt equally helpless. There was nothing she could do to make it easier for him, nothing productive.

'I've got to get out of these clothes,' he said tightly. 'I'll go have a shower. Would you mind if I left the phone to ring here until I'm out?'

'No, of course not. Have you had dinner yet?'

He frowned. 'No, I forgot.'

'I'll fix you something. Come on up when you're ready.'

He looked at her, taking in her robe and damply curling hair. 'You were going to bed,' he said. 'I don't want to keep you up.'

'I won't be able to sleep, Bryant.'

He gazed at her, then nodded. 'I won't be long.'

Being preoccupied, she hadn't thought of putting on

some clothes, but she went into the bedroom now and slipped on jeans and her favorite brandy-colored sweater, then went to the kitchen.

She surveyed the contents of the refrigerator, deciding that she'd fix him a frittata. She could offer him food and company. It wasn't much, but it was something, she supposed. Being alone at a time like this had to be awful. She could only guess at the thoughts and feelings swamping him now.

She was happy to have something to do, and cooking calmed her. She chopped an onion and fried it, adding some left-over potatoes and vegetables and a cut-up tomato, then pouring beaten eggs over the mixture in the pan and spicing it all up with some herbs and grated cheese. She managed to turn the thing over without making a mess and when it was all cooked through it smelled delicious and looked beautiful.

Bryant came back wearing jeans and a sweater and looking dry and clean, but his eyes had a wild and worried look in them and her heart went out to him. She put her arms around him and held him, not knowing what to say, saying nothing. His arms came around her, holding her so tight it was almost hard to breathe. The wool of his sweater was soft against her cheek and she could hear the thumping of his heart.

'I've got something for you to eat,' she said at last, and he released her. He ate in silence, his thoughts not on the food in front of him. She made a fresh pot of coffee, willing the phone to ring.

She put a cup of coffee in front of him and sat down at the table. 'I thought of something,' she said, feeling her heart beat nervously. 'I need to ask you a question.'

His eyes met hers. 'All right.'

'What happened to your...to Paul's mother?' She swallowed nervously. 'Did she die?'

His face went rigid. 'No.'

He wasn't looking at her and she took a deep breath. 'Where is she?'

'I have no idea.' His tone was clipped and cold.

She glanced at his hands, noticing the tight grasp of his fingers around his knife and fork. 'Is there any possibility that Paul went to her?'

His laugh was short and caustic. 'No.' He picked up his cup and took a swallow of coffee.

She wanted to ask why he was so sure, but decided not to. She looked at him silently.

He set the cup down. 'She took off when Paul was just a baby.' His voice was icy and Zoe felt a shiver go down her spine.

'I'm...sorry,' she said, the words coming out with difficulty.

He got up and stood in front of the window, looking out. The silence throbbed with tension and unspoken questions.

'I came home from work one day and found her packing,' he said tonelessly, his back turned to her. 'The bed was covered with clothes. Boxes of her things were everywhere—books, music tapes, artwork, kitchen stuff, everything. She was moving out with everything she owned. She'd had enough, she said. I asked her, Enough of what? and she said, "Enough of everything".' He paused. 'She said she had better things to do with her time.'

'Better things than what?'

'Taking care of a baby.'

Zoe's heart contracted. 'She left the baby?' she whispered.

He turned to look at her. His face worked. There was something terrible in his eyes. 'Yes. She said to me, "You wanted him, you take care of him."'

Zoe stared at him. 'She didn't want her own baby?'

'No. The pregnancy was...not planned. She wanted an abortion and I persuaded her not to.'

'Why?'

'Because it was *my* child we were talking about. *My* son or daughter, and not accepting responsibility because it was not *convenient* was a selfish, rotten excuse. There was no good reason, in my book, why we couldn't have a child. I was sure that she'd come around. I thought her maternal feelings would develop once the shock was over.'

'And they didn't?'

'No. Not even after he was born.'

It seemed unimaginable, but it happened; she knew that much. 'Oh, God, what a tragedy.'

'Yes.'

'What did you feel about all this?'

He laughed bitterly. 'I stopped loving her. I think I never really loved her in the first place. I was taken by her personality. She was fun and exciting and amusing and sexy, all that stuff that looks so nice on the outside—wrappings and ribbons. But not until she got pregnant did I realize that there was nothing below the surface, that she really only lived for herself, that she had no sense of responsibility and no strength of character.' He shrugged. 'I was foolish not to have seen that earlier, but I was young and thought myself in love and perhaps I subconsciously didn't *want* to see it.' The lines by the side of his mouth deepened in a grimace. 'God knows the mind works in strange ways.'

'What did you do after she walked out?'

'I took care of my son. I raised him.' His mouth twisted bitterly. 'Not very successfully, it appears.'

Her heart ached for him. 'Oh, Bryant, Paul is a great kid! He has problems, but so do lots of kids. It will all get worked out.'

'He ran away from home, from me.' His voice was raw with distress and the words cut through her. They held a wealth of meaning, a wealth of pain.

He loves him, she thought. He raised him by himself, doing what he thought was right, and now this.

She had never felt so helpless in her life. She moved over and put her arms around him. She couldn't think of anything else to do. Everything will be all right, she wanted to say, but stopped the words. They were clichéd, hollow. She had no power to make that promise.

The phone rang. They both jumped. She grabbed the receiver, her heart thumping.

It was Maxie inviting her to a seminar on the communication with the higher self. Zoe swallowed a hysterical little laugh as she half listened to Maxie mentioning things about souls and mirrors and divinity.

'I'm having trouble enough with my lower self right now, Maxie,' she said, 'and why are you calling so late? It's past eleven!'

'Oh, is it?'' Maxie sounded surprised. 'I didn't even notice the time. I'm sorry, did I wake you up?'

'No, no, it's all right.' She glanced over at Bryant, hesitating for a moment. 'Bryant is here. We're worried about Paul. He hasn't come home.'

'Oh, my God,' whispered Maxie. 'I saw him leave this afternoon.'

Wild hope flooded her. 'You saw him leave? When?' From the corner of her eye she saw Bryant leap to his feet and make for the phone in the kitchen.

'About four-thirty,' said Maxie. 'A limousine picked him up.'

For the second time she swallowed a hysterical little laugh. Here she was worried about him walking the streets of DC in the rain and wind, cold, hungry, afraid.

He had not just walked away, carrying his bag, for parts unknown. He had done it with class. He had left in a limo. Oh, God.

'Did you see anybody? Was he with somebody?' came Bryant's voice, clipped, businesslike. Zoe decided to leave the questioning up to him.

'There was another kid,' said Maxie.

'What did he look like?'

Maxie groaned. 'I don't know! I didn't pay any attention. A kid. A boy.'

'How big?'

'I don't know. Bigger than Paul. I can't remember a thing about him. I'm sorry, so sorry.'

'What about the limousine?' asked Bryant. 'What kind was it?'

'Silver-gray. Classy.'

All limousines were classy as far as Zoe was concerned. There was nothing more Maxie could tell them and Zoe felt defeated as she hung up the phone.

Neither she nor Bryant had any idea who the boy or the owner of the gray limo could have been. Fear kept growing inside her as the minutes went by and then the phone rang again, startling her so much that she spilled coffee on her jean leg.

A woman's voice asked for Mr Sinclair. Zoe handed him the phone.

'Bryant Sinclair,' he said into the receiver. Then he was silent as he listened, and suddenly he closed his eyes and all tension drained from his face.

'No, I didn't know,' he said. 'I appreciate your calling me.' Silence. 'If it doesn't inconvenience you...'

Zoe buried her face in her hands, feeling shaky with relief. This was about Paul; it had to be. She heard Bryant replace the receiver and felt him sit down next to her.

'He's in Richmond.'

She jerked her head up. '*Richmond*? What's he doing there?'

'Spending the weekend with one of his schoolfriends.'

'One of his friends? In Richmond? That's an hour away!'

'The kid's mother lives there. His parents are divorced and he lives in DC with his father during the week and visits his mother on the weekends. Paul went along for the weekend. Apparently this Steve brings friends now and then but his mother got suspicious because I hadn't even called to verify the invitation, and she overheard the boys talking about Paul running away, so she decided to check things out.'

'Smart woman.' She bit her lip. 'Now what?'

'I'll go get him tomorrow. She offered to have him stay the night since it's late and the weather is getting worse.' He rubbed his face, as if to wipe away the remnants of worry. 'Paul doesn't know she called. She's afraid that if she says anything he'll take off before I get there.'

Zoe let out a deep sigh. 'I'm so relieved.' Then with a sudden burst of energy she jumped up and laughed. 'Well, we should celebrate! He's alive and well.'

'Until I get my hands on him. If he ever, ever tries something like this again...'

She stopped in front of him and frowned down at him.

'Tell me all you are is mad. Tell me you don't feel just the tiniest bit of relief.'

A smile tugged at his mouth. He was relieved all right—it was there in his face, in the smile playing around his mouth. The light was back in his eyes and he looked ten years younger. And—she felt her pulse leap—very…appealing.

His mouth quirked. 'Okay, Counselor, I'm relieved. A tiny little bit.'

'Hah!' she said, and swung away to the kitchen to pour them each a glass of wine.

She'd barely sat down again when the phone rang for the fifth time that night. With her free hand she lifted the receiver to her ear. 'Hello?'

'Ms Langdon, it's Paul.' His voice sounded low and strange, as if he was nervous and he didn't want to be overheard. Her heart leaped.

'Paul!' she said in surprise. Bryant's head snapped up.

'I know it's late and everything, but I gotta talk to you. I don't know what to do!'

Bryant moved over to take the receiver from her, but she swiftly moved away from his grasp and shook her head.

'You don't know what to do about what?' she said to Paul.

'I ran away and my dad doesn't know where I am and I'm too scared to call him. He's gonna kill me.'

She took a deep breath, her gaze on Bryant. 'I don't think he's going to kill you, Paul. He's been worried about you. We've all been worried about you,' she added.

'It was a stupid thing to do. I got to talking about wanting to run away with Steve. He said he's run away lots of times and he came up with this plan and…and…I

was mad at my dad and so I thought...' His voice
faded out.

'What plan was that?'

'That I should go with him to his mother's house in
Richmond and then on Sunday he'd help me get on a
bus to Miami and from there I was gonna sneak on a
plane to Argentina. He'd read a book and he said he
knew how to do it. We looked at a map and everything.'

'And you've changed your mind?'

'I never should've listened to him! It's a stupid idea!'
He made a little choking sound. 'And I lied to my
grandma too,' he added in a barely audible whisper.

'I know. But you're safe now,' she said. 'Where's
Steve?'

'He's asleep. And his mom's in the bedroom with the
TV on so I snuck to the kitchen to call you. I couldn't
sleep. I kept thinking about Dad. I love my dad, Ms
Langdon. He just makes me feel so bad sometimes. Now
I don't know what to do!' He was close to tears. 'I'm
sorry, Ms Langdon. I'm so sorry.'

She felt a lump in her throat. 'I think you should tell
your father that yourself, Paul.'

'I'm scared.'

'Yes, of course you are, but do you remember we
talked about taking responsibility for our own actions?'

'Yes,' he mumbled. 'But I was hoping...I thought
maybe you'd explain how it was to him first, and then
when I tell him maybe he won't be so mad.'

Her heart swelled. He trusted her. He needed her. 'All
right, I'll do that.'

She heard his sigh of relief and smiled. 'Thank you.
You're the best!' He swallowed audibly. 'And can you
tell him I'm in Richmond and that I don't know how to
get home?'

Zoe almost laughed. He'd been scheming to go to Argentina, a foreign country on another continent. Now he was an hour out of Washington and he didn't know how to get back home. 'How did you get to Richmond this afternoon?'

'Steve's dad has a limo with a driver. It was cool.'

'And the driver just let you come along?'

'Steve's allowed to take friends. He does all the time.'

'I see. Well, I'll tell your dad.'

'Will you tell him now? I mean, you won't wait till morning, will you?'

'I'll tell him right away. You'd better give me the phone number so he can call Steve's mother for directions.' She wrote it down and told him goodnight. Replacing the receiver, she looked at Bryant, whose face was livid.

'That was your son suffering from great pangs of guilt, worry and remorse.' She took a drink of her wine.

Bryant's jaw hardened. 'It's just as well he's all the way in Richmond and I have time to cool off. I'd give him a hiding he would never forget, otherwise.'

'It wouldn't help the situation,' she said, then bit her tongue.

He gave her a long look, then closed his eyes. 'No, I suppose you're right. I suppose what I should do is talk to him and try to understand him.'

'Bryant, I think you do understand him.'

He was silent. Then he jumped up.

'Do you have any idea what it felt like?' he said fiercely. 'To have her walk out on me? To be alone with a baby whose mother didn't want him? I went through hell! I vowed I'd do anything to make him happy, to make him feel loved, to make him tough so he'd never have to feel the way I did!'

Her legs were trembling as she listened to his words. It was so clear now what had happened between them, so clear what Bryant wanted for his son. He didn't want his son to hurt, to feel pain. He'd wanted to protect him. There was a tightness in her chest and a terrible feeling of remorse for having misunderstood him. She of all people should have known better. He loved his son; how could she have doubted it?

She saw him control his emotions with a visible effort. He looked at her. 'But I can't tell him not to feel the way he does, can I?'

She swallowed. 'No.'

He groaned. 'God, I screwed this up.'

She gave a shaky smile, feeling suddenly overwhelmed with love, a shivering, trembling, joyous feeling. 'So fix it.'

He glanced back at her, offering a lopsided smile. 'Is that your professional advice?'

She felt herself begin to smile. 'I think it's called common sense.'

'That's good. I can deal with common sense.'

'How about another glass of wine?'

'I can deal with that too.'

The air seemed lighter, easier to breathe, as if a heavy fog had lifted. Paul was all right. Everything would work out fine. She felt like dancing, but with the two glasses of wine in her hand she had to control her impulse. She was aware of the silly grin on her face as she came back into the room.

She handed him his glass but he put it down on the table, then took hers and set it down as well. He pulled her down next to him on the sofa and took her hands.

'Thank you,' he said, and smiled at her. It was the most wonderful sight, that smile, and that bright blue light in his eyes that sent shivers of something delicious sparking along her nerves.

'I didn't do anything.'

'Oh, yes, you did. You were here.' He put his arms around her and drew her close. 'And you fixed me dinner and you listened and you didn't criticize and you smell very nice,' he said close to her ear. Then his mouth was warm on her neck, trailing across her cheek to her mouth.

'I'm glad you're feeling better,' she said breathlessly, feeling the warmth of his back beneath her hands—such a wonderful, strong, muscled back.

'I'm feeling much better.' He trailed the tip of his tongue along the contours of her lips. 'As a matter of fact, I'm beginning to feel positively, dangerously wonderful.'

Her heart lurched. 'Me too,' she whispered.

His hands tangled in her hair. 'Is there any reason why we shouldn't feel so wonderful?' She heard the smile in his voice.

'No,' she whispered back, feeling a storm of need wash over her, sweet and hot and unstoppable.

His mouth stroked her lips, teasing, tantalizing. 'I'd better go downstairs first,' he murmured, his breath warm against her cheek, 'to get what we need.'

She tightened her arms around him. She did not want him to go. 'Don't go,' she whispered. 'I have what we need.'

There was the shortest silence. 'You do?'

She nodded, eyes closed. 'The way you've been kissing me gave me all kinds of ideas.'

A soft chuckle. 'You were supposed to.'

'I guess I passed the test.'

'You are a smart woman. And very sexy.' His hands

slipped under her sweater to her breast, caressing, teasing through the lace of her bra. 'Do you know how very sexy you are?' he murmured.

She was flooded with a tingling warmth. It was hard to think, to talk. 'No,' she whispered. 'Tell me all about it.'

He laughed softly. 'I'll do better. I'll show you.'

CHAPTER SIX

BRYANT took Zoe's face in his hands, a wonderful, gentle gesture, and smiled at her—a sensuous smile that quickened her pulse. 'Your eyes are the color of cognac,' he said. 'Very intoxicating.'

He bent his head toward her and she closed her eyes. He laughed softly, stroking his lips lightly across each eyelid. 'You can't hide now,' he said; 'it's too late.'

She let the sweet sensations flow over her, not resisting, just letting it happen.

He slid his hands to the back of her neck, burying them in her hair. 'And what sort of ideas did you get from the way I kissed you?' he asked.

'I have a rich imagination,' she said recklessly.

'You're not answering my question.'

'I can't remember,' she murmured. 'I can't think.'

'Maybe if I kiss you it'll come back.' His mouth closed over hers and she kissed him back, warmth radiating through her at the taste and feel of him.

Breathless moments later, he drew back, meeting her eyes. 'I want to see you,' he said raggedly. 'All of you.' The words rippled through her drunkenly, and she felt him lift her up and carry her out of the room and into her bedroom where he set her down on her feet. With quick expertise, he slipped the sweater off over her head and took off her bra.

'Ah, beautiful,' he said softly, sliding his hands lightly

from her shoulders down her arms, a warm feathering
along her skin that made her tingle. His eyes, a dark,
sultry blue, looked into hers. Then, carefully, gently, he
cupped her breasts in his big hands and stroked her nip-
ples with his thumbs.

She caught her breath as sparks of electricity jolted
through her. Her legs felt rubbery and threatened to
buckle. Closing her eyes, she leaned into him, feeling
the soft wool of his sweater against her bare skin. His
hands moved to her jeans and stripped them down over
her hips and thighs, taking her panties right along with
them. He lowered her to the bed and moments later he
joined her, his clothes gone. She felt dizzy with his near-
ness—the warmth of his skin, the clean male scent of
him.

Leaning on one elbow, he looked down at her with a
faint smile and his free hand began to explore her body,
slowly, sensuously. 'You feel wonderful,' he said in a
low, husky voice. 'Soft and warm and smooth.'

In answer, a wordless sound came from her mouth
and she reached out to him, wanting to touch him too,
but he caught her hand. 'Not yet,' he said, and went on
caressing her with magic, tantalizing fingers as she lay
there, savoring the delights, aching to feel him too,
yearning.

'How's this?' he whispered. 'Was this one of your
imaginings?'

'Yes,' she whispered.

'And this?'

'Yes.' Her room was no longer just her room, her bed
no longer just her bed. It was a place of magic where
time and thought did not exist, where all that mattered
were the wondrous sensations and intimate delights of
love.

'And this?' he murmured, kissing soft, sensitive places, making her body throb. 'Was this in your fantasies?'

'Yes.' It was a sigh. She squirmed restlessly against him, wanting him, needing him, doing an exploration of her own, relishing the feel of his strong, muscled body under her hands.

'Zoe…' Her name was a moan. He slid his body over hers, and his mouth came down on hers again, full of heat and hunger. Again and again they touched and kissed and stroked until she thought she would go mad with the need pulsing through her.

A wildness took hold of her, and she urged him closer. It was good and right, supremely right to feel so close to him, to give him everything she had, not to hold back. Their bodies fit together beautifully, created, it seemed, for this exquisite pleasure of loving each other. She could no longer think, could only feel the sweet delirium as passion swept her away and the turbulence of ancient rhythms claimed them both.

She held him tight, trembling in the aftermath, not wanting to let go. He slumped against her, breathing raggedly. She kissed the soft, damp skin of his neck, curling her hands through his hair. A peaceful languor stole over her as her heart calmed down and her breathing returned to normal.

'Bryant?' she said softly.

He made a low, inarticulate sound, not moving.

'It was better than any of my fantasies,' she whispered. 'In case you were wondering.'

He raised his head, his mouth curving in amusement. 'And you are a wonderful, loving, sexy woman,' he said huskily. He kissed her with infinite tenderness and her heart filled with love.

They fell asleep, holding each other. Once, late in the night, she came semi-awake, vaguely conscious of him in the bed with her. Reaching out her hand, she searched for him, touching his chest. He stirred, muttering softly, drawing her back into his arms. She nestled against him, sighing.

They made love again—slowly, sleepily, deliciously.

In the morning she awoke to find him next to her, watching her.

'Good morning,' he said.

'Morning,' she said huskily, overwhelmed by the enormity of the feelings rushing through her suddenly. Pale winter light filtered through the curtains. She closed her eyes, feeling his hand stroking her cheek as he gently moved her hair out of her face.

'I made coffee,' he said. 'Would you like a cup?'

She opened one eye. 'You were up already?'

His mouth curved. 'You never stirred. You were sleeping the sleep of the innocent.'

'I must have been very tired.'

He chuckled. 'I hope our frolicking wasn't too much for you?'

Frolicking. She laughed into the pillow. 'I'll live, and yes, I would like a cup of coffee.'

He brought two mugs and got back into bed beside her. She sipped the hot brew gratefully, thinking how nice it was of him not to disappear the moment he woke up.

'What time is it?' she asked, too lazy to turn her head and look at the clock on her bedside table.

'Just after eight.'

The coffee revived her and cleared her head. She remembered again the long, frightening evening they'd spent worrying about Paul. Paul, who was in Richmond, delivered there by limo.

'When do you have to leave to go to Richmond to get Paul?' she asked, hoping selfishly that it wasn't within the next hour or so.

'In a couple of hours.'

She thought of Paul and what Bryant had told her, and an idea formed in her mind. Maybe it had been there all along and was just surfacing into her consciousness now. It was a good idea, and she wondered why it had not come to her earlier.

'What are you thinking?' he asked, playing with her fingers.

'I have an idea.' She met his eyes. 'I'd like Paul to come here after school until you come home.'

He shifted the pillow behind his back and shook his head. 'I can't ask that of you, Zoe.'

'You aren't asking. I'm offering.' Her eyes were on his bare chest. A wonderful chest, solid and strong. She raised her gaze to his face. 'I'd like it, really. You'd have to ask him, of course; he may not want it.'

He gave a short laugh. 'You know he likes being here. Besides, he'll do anything not to have to deal with Kristin.'

She put her hand on his chest, feeling the steady beat of his heart under her hands. 'She seems rather a friendly, cheerful person,' she said lightly, aware of a faint sense of guilt. She wanted to know what Bryant thought of Kristin, a question she would never, ever ask him in a more straightforward way.

He put his hands behind his head and groaned. 'Relentlessly peppy. It grates on my nerves, to tell you the truth.'

Why did she feel relief? She should be ashamed of

herself. Zoe smiled. 'Then let her go. Maybe this will lessen the tension between you and Paul. You're in a power struggle, Bryant, and there are no winners in those.'

He frowned, considering. She watched him, trying to read his face. He hesitated, then, 'All right, let's give it a try,' he said, caving in, 'but I want to pay you.'

She didn't want to be paid. He insisted, saying he had no intention of taking advantage of her. She said he wouldn't be because it was her idea in the first place. He said he'd feel like it.

She sighed dramatically. 'Okay, pay me, if that would make you feel better.'

'It would make me feel better.'

She threw a pillow at him. He threw a pillow at her. Then they made love again, playful, laughing, sliding off the bed and ending up on the floor.

'I have another idea,' she said later, back in bed.

'Breakfast,' he said.

'No.'

'I'm starved.'

'You can starve just a little longer. I want you to hear my idea.'

He turned and put his face against her breasts. 'I suppose I have no choice.'

'None whatsoever.' She stroked the back of his head.

He gave a long-suffering sigh. 'All right, tell me your other brilliant idea.'

'I think you should call Kako's parents in Argentina and see if they'd consider sending their son over here for a while during the summer. Then you take both the guys to the Epcot Center at Disney World, and to the beach, or whatever they want.'

He was silent.

'Bryant, you can't expect Paul to forget about his friend, to accept he'll never see him again. He isn't dead and buried, you know.'

'I know, I know,' he said, his voice muffled against her breast.

'You should applaud his loyalty. They've been writing letters back and forth regularly. That's not standard behavior for twelve-year-old boys, believe me.'

He raised his head. 'All right, I'll call. I'll see what I can do.'

She smiled, and he frowned at her. 'Don't look so smug.'

'I'm not smug. It still may not work out, but I hope so. It will make Paul so happy.' She threw the sheet off. 'Now I'll fix us some breakfast.'

'Don't let your liberated sisters hear you say that,' he said. 'They might think you're being servile.'

She grinned. 'Oh, really? Well, liberation is about choice. I choose, out of my very own free will, to cook breakfast for the man who shared my bed last night. And what's more I'll even enjoy doing it.'

He lay back, hands behind his head, and gave her a lazy grin. 'I like your kind of liberation.'

She glowered at him. 'Don't you get any ideas.'

She had no trouble fixing breakfast for a man. A man in her house, a man in her bed. Not just any man, of course. She puttered in the kitchen, humming a song, feeling happy.

It didn't last long.

She was pouring coffee when Bryant entered the kitchen, a towel around his waist, Nick's letter with the cartoon illustrations in his hand.

'Who's this guy Nick?' he asked, his voice devoid of all expression.

She stared at him, flooded by outrage. 'Were you reading my mail?'

His jaw went rigid. 'No, I was not reading your mail. This letter was lying on that little table in full view, with this huge red heart and "I LOVE YOU!" scrawled all over it. It rather jumped up at me.'

It had been there all yesterday evening and he'd never noticed it. He'd had other things on his mind then.

'Nick is a friend,' she said, trying to stay calm. She stirred her coffee, her heart sinking.

'A friend who writes you love-letters,' he stated coolly. 'Interesting.'

Oh, damn. How was she going to explain this? 'He doesn't write me love-letters. He was just being...funny, fantasizing, joking, whatever you want to call it.'

He tossed the letter on to the counter, but it slipped off. Pages fluttered to the floor. The full-page tent drawing, the two of them clutching at each other, lay there like an accusation. For a moment there was a pregnant silence. Then he bent to retrieve the drawing and studied it. There was no mistaking who the woman was in the tent clutching the man. It was her, and he would recognize her easily.

'How cozy,' he said caustically. 'And this is supposed to be a joke too?'

She clenched her jaw. 'Yes.'

'And what kind of a joke is this?'

She felt suddenly deadly depressed. Everything was ruined—the atmosphere, the sense of love and joy. She wanted to cry. 'Just read the letter and you'll see,' she said dully. She felt deflated.

'I don't want to read the damn letter! I want you to explain to me what this is all about!'

'I don't owe you any explanations, Bryant!'

'Like hell you don't!'

She stared at him standing there, bare-chested, hands on his towel-clad hips, face radiating self-righteous outrage—as if he owned the place, as if he owned her. She fought her own sense of outrage and lost miserably.

'Just because we made love it doesn't mean you own me!' she said, her voice shaking. 'Who the hell do you think you are?'

'I'm a man who doesn't sleep with women who are involved with other men!' he bit out.

How commendable, she wanted to say sarcastically, but swallowed the words. It was commendable, after all.

'I'm not involved with other men.' Her legs were shaking. 'Not sexually and not romantically. Nick and I are friends, that's all. We worked in the same school in Cameroon and after I left we started writing letters.' She sat down at the table and took a drink of her coffee to fortify her. 'He said he was lonely. I said I was lonely too.' Her voice shook and she took another drink of coffee. 'He suggested we get married because we were both lonely, and for me to come back to Africa.'

'And that's a joke?' His eyes bored into hers.

'He wasn't being serious, Bryant! At least, not all the way. Mostly he was joking.'

'Would you want to marry him?'

How could he even ask such a thing? She stared at him, and tears burned behind her eyes. 'No,' she said, and her throat felt raw.

'Why not, if you're such good friends?'

'Being friends alone isn't enough. There's no...magic between us.'

No magic, as there was between the two of them—this indefinable attraction, the pull, the desire, the sweetness that made your heart race.

There was a silence. She looked at him and he looked at her, and then the tears flooded her eyes and ran down her cheeks.

He moved two giant steps, pulled her up and into his arms and buried his face in her hair. 'I'm sorry,' he said huskily. 'I'm a stupid bastard. I don't know what got over me.' He kissed her eyes, then gently wiped the tears away with his thumbs. 'But you probably do, don't you, Counselor?'

'So do you,' she said, and swallowed fiercely at the constriction in her throat.

'Tell me.'

She dragged in a shaky breath. 'You spent half the night making love to me and the first thing you saw when you got up was another man's letter with a big heart and "I LOVE YOU!" scrawled all across the bottom and a drawing of him and me in bed together. It was like a slap in the face and your manly pride was wounded.'

He groaned. 'Temporary insanity. A momentary lapse. I'm over it. I've got my normal arrogant, macho male confidence back.' He kissed her—a long, lingering, loving kiss that banished the hurt and anger and made her heart dance and sing. She wound her arms around his neck and leaned into him. It was there again, that irresistible pull, that tingling in her blood.

'Magic,' he whispered.

Zoe was stirring a big pot of Hungarian goulash, rich with large chunks of beef and fragrant with garlic and onions and paprika, wondering if Bryant would like it. She glanced at the clock on her microwave oven. He'd be home soon.

Home. She grinned at herself. Shame on her. She was

acting like a wife, cooking dinner and waiting for her man to return home.

Well, what was wrong with that? Nothing, nothing at all. As a matter of fact she would do this for the rest of her life, if with a few modifications in the general design of things.

Every day, after school, Paul came up to her apartment, and he seemed happy to do so. Ever since the day he had run away, the situation had changed for the better. When Bryant had told him that Kako would come and stay for a while during the summer, he had been beside himself with joy and excitement.

Everything suddenly was happy and joyful. They'd fallen into a happy routine of Bryant coming up to her apartment when he returned from work and the three of them eating together. She enjoyed cooking for them; it was so much more satisfying than preparing something to eat for herself only. It was obvious to her that both Bryant and Paul enjoyed being with her in her cozy apartment, and did not at all object to her domestic ways. In fact, they seemed to search it out, and had trouble leaving.

Maybe it was what they needed—a little togetherness, a little female companionship. It was what she needed—togetherness, companionship, love, a sense of belonging.

She couldn't help thinking sometimes how nice it would be if it could be a more permanent situation. Maybe Bryant would decide to settle down, in spite of his plans to move overseas again. Maybe he would ask her to marry him.

Ah, such lovely, romantic dreams! But then, she was in quite a lovely, romantic mood these days.

So she went on fantasizing—about being married to Bryant, about having a family, a brother or sister for

Paul. She would look at the two of them at her table and
feel her heart swell with love. On the nights when Paul
stayed overnight at his grandparents' house, or a
friend's, she and Bryant would go out—to dinner, to a
party, to the theater. And afterward they'd go up to her
place and make a fire in the fireplace and make love.

There was nothing better than to wake up on a quiet
winter morning next to Bryant, warm and snug under
the covers. Nothing better than to feel his arms draw her
close against him, feeling delicious desire curl itself lazily through her sleepy limbs, knowing she loved him,
knowing she would love him forever.

Oh, the joys of the Christmas season! She loved it all.
People shopping everywhere, music, glitter, color, and
smiles. packages, pretty wrapping paper and shiny ribbons. Hot, spiced cider on a cold night. On top of all
that she was in love. It made everything more beautiful,
more cheerful—life sprinkled with gold dust.

The three of them would have Christmas at her apartment. Bryant's parents had accepted an invitation to
spend the holiday season with old friends in Switzerland,
which meant they would not have a family Christmas
dinner at their house, as had been a tradition. Even when
living in Argentina, Bryant had taken Paul to
Washington at Christmas time to be with his family.

'We can have Christmas here,' Zoe had offered
promptly, feeling a little guilty for being relieved. She'd
met his parents and had had dinner at their house, which
was more like a historic mansion full of priceless an-
tiques than a family home.

Bryant's father looked as if he could have walked
straight out of an English castle. He was tall and
aristocratic-looking and emanated waves of polite re-

serve. He moved with a minimum of body motion, as if he was under superb control of every little muscle in his body at all times. His eyes were the same vivid blue as his son's and seemed to miss nothing.

Bryant's mother was a lady. A nice lady, for sure, but not the kind you'd throw your arms around for a warm hug. Zoe liked people you could hug.

Christmas morning found the three of them around a crackling fire, opening gifts. Too many gifts. Small ones, large ones, funny ones. The one Zoe liked best was the Thai cookbook Bryant gave her. 'For the woman who gives me fire and spice and everything nice,' he had written inside. She felt warm all over as she read the words and looking up she met his eyes, which glimmered with secret humor.

Later they helped her get ready for dinner. The apartment smelled deliciously of roasting turkey. A cranberry and apple pie sat on the counter in the kitchen, the table was set, the candles were lit.

They sat around the table and ate. Everything was perfect, everything was delicious. Zoe looked around the table at the two of them, feeling her heart overflow.

It was a perfect Christmas.

Slowly, insidiously, things became less perfect. There was nothing specific Zoe could put her finger on, just a faint apprehension that something wasn't quite right. She tried to push the feeling away and went on dreaming her dreams.

January brought icy winds and frigid temperatures and February wasn't much better. After several years in the tropics, she'd longed for winter—sitting in front of a roaring fire, wearing cozy knit sweaters, drinking hot chocolate, walking in fresh snow. But now it had been enough and she wanted spring to come—flowers, warm sunshine. Restlessness stirred in her blood. Restlessness and a nameless fear.

Bryant called late one night when he was working at home and asked her to come down and help him out. She was already in her nightgown, ready for bed, and was surprised by his request. She put on a robe and slippers and skipped down the stairs.

He opened the door almost immediately. He still wore his business clothes, but the jacket and tie were gone, and the sleeves of his shirt were rolled up. His hair was disheveled and he looked tired.

'Help you out with what?' she asked as he closed the door behind her.

'I've been working on this project proposal and my brain is mush. I'd like you to listen, give me some feedback, ideas, thoughts, whatever comes to mind.'

Zoe frowned. 'What kind of project?'

'It's an enormous civil engineering project in Brazil. It's interesting but there are problems with the integration of the project components and there's been too little—'

'I don't know anything about civil engineering projects, Bryant.'

He waved his hand in dismissal. 'You've lived in developing countries and you know people and you didn't let me finish. Another big problem with the planning is that there's been far too little socio-anthropological work done, which is incredibly irresponsible.'

'You don't usually think of civil engineering and social anthropology in the same breath,' she said, 'but come to think of it I don't suppose you plunk roads and dams and power plants in the middle of people's living environment and leave them unaffected.'

'Exactly.' He nudged her toward the sofa. 'Now sit down and listen.'

She sat down and listened.

There was no doubt that he was enthusiastic, in spite of his many misgivings. As she listened, it also became obvious that running this massive project was just the thing for him to be doing, the perfect next assignment.

As he went on talking, it was clear that this was what he had in mind—for Paul and him to go to Brazil.

A knot of apprehension formed in her throat. Looking down at her hands, she noticed they were clasped tightly in her lap. She relaxed them, massaging her fingers, and, feeling suddenly at a loss as to what to do with them, she crossed her arms in front of her chest.

'If your company wins the contract for this project, when would you leave?' She could not help but ask the question.

'Not until August or September. This will never get finalized before then. Besides, I'd want Paul to finish the school year here first.' He folded the map of Brazil that lay spread out on the coffee-table in front of them. 'It's a long shot. This may never work out, and I won't go unless some drastic changes are made.' His gaze was directed at the papers on the table, not at her. She studied the strong, clean lines of his profile, feeling the apprehension grow.

'Paul's doing much better in school these days,' she said carefully. 'He finally seems to have settled down.'

'Yes. Thanks to you.' He came to his feet and rubbed the back of his neck.

She swallowed hard, looking up at him. 'Bryant, I'm concerned that pulling him away and starting over again somewhere new is not such a good idea.'

His face stiffened. 'I have a career to manage and a

job to do, Zoe. He'll be all right this time.' His voice was calm, but she sensed the tension behind the words, saw the tension in his body. She regretted having said anything, having stirred up the old conflict.

'I know. I'm sorry. It's not my business. I'm not his mother.'

He said nothing, as if he hadn't heard her.

She stared at the pattern of the Turkish rug on the floor, the bright colors blurring before her eyes. She heard the ticking of the old clock on the wall, oddly loud.

Would you like to be Paul's mother? How natural it would be for him to ask that question, but he did not.

How stupid of her to think this way. What made her assume that his dreams were the same as hers? That he wanted out of life what she wanted out of it?

Outside, somewhere in the distance, a police siren began to wail. Then another siren joined in. An ambulance? She shivered suddenly.

A terrible fear overwhelmed her—a foreboding, a sense of doom. She kept staring at the rug, not moving, listening to the sirens coming closer.

CHAPTER SEVEN

ZOE hadn't wanted to admit it, but they didn't talk about the future.

Not a promising sign.

They talked about lots of other things—important things, trivial things, happy and sad things—but not about the future. She knew his opinions and philosophies about many issues. She knew he was a dynamic, interesting, sexy man who loved his son and took his work seriously, but she did not know his deeper, intimate feelings, and she did not know where she fit into his future.

How could she not have seen the signs?

She raised her head slowly. Bryant was concentrating on a paper in his hand. His face looked tired, with deep lines etched beside his mouth. It was a face she loved and she had seen it smiling, amused, angry, reserved. What dreams were hidden behind that face? She didn't know. How could she not know?

Bryant tossed the paper on to the table. 'How about a glass of wine?' He moved toward the kitchen.

'Yes, thanks.'

She rubbed her face, trying to erase negative thoughts. Be positive, she told herself. Time's on your side. We're talking August or September—it's months away yet.

He came back from the kitchen and handed her a glass.

'Why have you never married again?' she asked, trying to sound casual. She had to start somewhere.

He shrugged. 'It never worked out that way.'

Maybe he hadn't loved anybody. Maybe he didn't love her.

No, no. How could he make love to her the way he did if he didn't love her? His loving was real—selfless and tender and passionate.

Maybe he needed time. Maybe marriage frightened him. A vision floated before her mind's eye—Bryant coming home, finding the house turned upside-down, his wife packing. She shook the image away and took a gulp of wine. His wife was another subject they did not discuss. Ever.

Bryant was busy clearing the table, stacking the papers and putting them aside.

'Don't stop on my account,' she said. 'I'll leave.'

'I don't want you to leave.' He took the glass from her hand and put it on the table. 'Come here,' he said softly.

She moved toward him and he put his arms around her and kissed her—a loving, passionate kiss that made tears come to her eyes. He must have felt the dampness on her cheek because he suddenly drew away a little and looked at her.

'Are you crying?' he said softly.

She swallowed and shook her head foolishly. 'I just…want you so much,' she whispered. It wasn't what she had wanted to say. I love you so much, had been on the tip of her tongue, but courage had failed her.

'I want you too.' He wound his fingers through her hair. 'I'm glad you came down to help me think,' he said against her lips. 'Very nice of you.'

'I'm a nice person,' she whispered, trying for a light note.

'I know. I don't deserve it.'

'True,' she murmured. 'I really should stop being nice to you.'

'You should, but please don't.'

'Okay.'

'You're easy.'

'Easy and nice. And foolish. A foolish, easy, nice person. There is no hope for me. I'm doomed.' Her voice was light, covering up the darkness inside.

'Doomed to what?'

'Bad stuff,' she whispered, trying not to give a name to whatever that might be. The sirens were only vaguely audible in the distance, fading, almost gone.

'I don't think so. Does this feel bad?' His hand had slipped inside her robe, and he was stroking her breast.

'No,' she murmured, feeling desire stir, feeling the world slip away as his mouth and hands made magic.

His kiss grew deeper and more urgent and she responded with a need of her own, her head light, her knees weak. He lifted her into his arms and carried her to his bedroom, locking the door behind them. He turned on the radio and soft, hypnotic jazz filled the air around them. He took off her robe and nightgown, bending to kiss each bare breast.

'You smell wonderful,' he said huskily, 'and I feel like a drowned rat.' He nudged her down on to the bed, put the covers over her and began stripping off his clothes. 'Stay put,' he said; 'I need a shower. I spent the afternoon in Foggy Bottom.'

She laughed softly. Discussing and negotiating at the State Department. Some of the work his company was involved in was full of political entanglements. How he loved dealing with politicians. She looked at this body, naked and aroused and beautiful, and it was difficult to breathe. She loved this man and she wanted nothing more now than to hold him close and love him.

I love you, she wanted to say, but something kept her from uttering the words—again. So many times she had wanted to say it and every time she swallowed the words, held back by an indefinable fear.

She closed her eyes. Don't think, she thought. Just feel.

She heard him move, felt his mouth touching hers. 'Don't go to sleep,' he said, amusement in his voice.

Warmth flooded her and she smiled. 'Not a chance.'

The bathroom door opened and closed. There was the faint sound of water running. She felt deliciously drowsy and warm with desire. The music curled around her heart. It was wonderful lying here waiting for him, anticipating. She heard him come back into the room not much later, then felt the movement of the bed as he slid in next to her. His hands were warm on her body, his mouth hot on hers. Mesmerizing delight, sweet fire. There was only the two of them now, in this softly lit room, the two of them together, surrounded by the sensuous sounds of the music—tempting, seducing.

Doubt was an ugly feeling. It crept insidiously through her thoughts, her mind, her blood, not diminished by the passing of the days. Sometimes in the middle of the day she would sit paralyzed at her desk and panic would overwhelm her.

He was going to leave.

He was going to leave just like that—without planning with her, without asking her if she wanted to come with him.

He was planning his life on his own because she did not belong in it.

'They're gonna think you're my mother,' said Paul as they walked home from school together one afternoon. Usually he walked home with a couple of kids living near by, or stayed after to play basketball.

'I suppose it's not very cool to walk home with your mother,' she said with a grin. She was well aware how easily children his age were embarrassed by their parents and how important it was to look cool.

'I wouldn't care,' he said, kicking a red pencil cap lying in the street. It was a sunny day in early March, with trees budding and bulbs poking hopefully out of the ground. Paul kept looking down, giving the pencil cap another kick.

'When I was little I used to want to have a mother, like the other kids,' he said.

She felt something twist inside her chest. 'But not any more?'

'Naw.' He shrugged carelessly, not looking at her. 'Besides, my dad isn't gonna marry again. That's what he said. We were talking about it the other day.'

Her heart stopped for a moment. She felt a sudden wild anger. It was true. Her suspicions were true. Bryant had no intention of making her part of his life.

She swallowed with difficulty, fighting for control, willing herself to come up with some response.

'Marriage is serious business,' she said then.

'I thought maybe you and him would get married.' He looked at her now, his serious blue-gray eyes almost hopeful.

'Why did you think that?'

He glanced away, embarrassed. ''Cos you...you like

each other and…and we're together a lot.' He swallowed. 'You're not like the other ones.'

'The other ones'. She stared blindly at the brick sidewalk. She didn't know if she could take more of this. She couldn't ask him about 'the other ones'—it would be wrong to question a child about his father's relationships with other women. But she could ask him about herself.

She pushed her hands deep into her coat pockets. 'Why am I different?' she asked casually.

He shrugged. 'You're more real. And…and you're nice to me—I mean, the others were nice too, but…' He gulped for air, struggling with the words. 'I think you're nice 'cos you like me.' The words had come rushing out as if he was afraid that courage might fail him halfway. He turned pink and looked away.

'I do like you. Is that so strange?'

'I dunno,' he mumbled.

'Well, I do know. It's not strange. I like you. I enjoy talking to you. It's not at all complicated.' She laughed. 'And I think you like me too.'

He looked up now. 'Yeah, of course I do!'

They turned the corner into their own street and walked the rest of the way in silence.

'My dad isn't gonna marry again. That's what he said'. The words haunted her through the rest of the day and all through a restless night. In the morning she dragged herself out of bed when her alarm went off, feeling exhausted. It was still dark outside her window and it had started raining in the night. It did not look like a promising day.

Not that there'd been any chance of that at all. She was going to talk to Bryant, confront him with her doubts and fears. Deal with the problem head-on. Tell him she was not some temporary playgirl and if he had no intention of making her part of his future she was no longer available for his present, either.

Oh, how brave she sounded. Her stomach churned with fear.

Two hours and several cups of coffee later she was sitting in her office conducting an anger-management workshop with a group of kids with behavioral problems. It was not one of her more successful sessions and she was relieved when the time was up and she could send them on to their next class. The kids gone, the quiet in her office was a balm for her aching head. The phone rang as she swallowed some aspirin with the cold dregs of coffee left in her cup.

Bryant. It was unusual for him to call her at her office and her heart leaped at the sound of his voice, then contracted at the thought of what she was going to tell him tonight.

'How about taking off the rest of the day?' he asked.

'A brilliant idea,' she said drily.

'Now and then I have one. How do you feel about being cosseted and pampered?'

'I'm all for it.' She rubbed her aching head.

'Excellent. I'll pick you up at the house in forty-five minutes.'

She put her coffee-cup down carefully. 'Taking the day off is a brilliant idea, but not one that I can put into action, Bryant.'

'Of course you can. You're a creative person; you'll find a way. Be ready in forty-five minutes.' He sounded very businesslike, very commanding. She wasn't sure if she liked it.

'Ready for what?' she asked.

'A surprise,' he said.

'How do I get ready for a surprise if I don't know what the surprise is?'

'You have a point there,' he said crisply. 'Pack a toothbrush, your swimsuit and your passport.'

'My *passport*?'

'You have one?'

'Yes! Of course I have one!'

'Good. I'll see you soon.'

'Bryant!' she wailed, but he had already hung up.

It was a dream, a delicious dream, and Zoe was afraid to open her eyes. Her body felt heavy with languor, but all her senses were wide awake—relishing the soft caress of the breeze on her sun-warmed skin, the powdery texture of the sand slipping through her fingers, the sensuous sound of the waves washing up on the beach.

Her mouth was still full of the sweetness of fresh mango and papaya she'd had for breakfast. She let out a soft sigh. Her body still remembered the touch of Bryant's hands, his mouth as they'd made love early this morning in a sunny room with wide-open windows.

It had to be a dream.

Carefully she opened her eyes a tiny bit. A brilliant blue sky stretched till the horizon where it met a shimmering, aquamarine sea. She sat up slowly, seeing Bryant walking out toward the water, going for a swim. Strong, muscled legs moved easily through the sand. The sun gleamed on his blond hair. Her heart made a joyous little leap. She was awake, she was sure of it, and this was no dream.

Yesterday at this time she'd been in her Washington office, with a cold rain pounding the windows, trying to persuade a bunch of wild children that bashing in each other's heads was not an acceptable way to solve problems. Now she was sitting on a tropical beach soaking up sunshine while listening to the rustle of palm-fronds and the gentle pounding of the surf, watching Bryant's sexy frame disappear into the sea.

Almost, almost, it had not happened. Almost she had not taken the day off. She'd sat in her office yesterday morning, the phone in her hand, wondering what made Bryant think he could order her around like some autocratic lord and master.

Then she'd rubbed her aching head some more, glanced out the window, seen the wet, naked trees, felt her feet, still cold and damp from sloshing through the rain, and thought, The hell with it, I'm ready for a surprise.

And a surprise it had been.

She hugged her sandy knees and grinned, remembering. A company limousine had taken her and Bryant to the airport, where they'd boarded a private company jet which had flown them straight to the island of Jamaica.

'*Jamaica*?' she'd asked, stunned, when he'd finally told her after take-off.

He'd waved his hand carelessly. 'Yes, you know, that island south of Cuba. Rum, reggae, Rastafarians.'

She'd glowered at him. 'I know where it is.'

He'd taken her hand, enveloping it in his own big one. 'Sit back, relax. I think you deserve a weekend of unadulterated cosseting and pampering. No cooking, no work, no babysitting.'

She wasn't going to argue with that. She'd tried to relax, which hadn't been easy considering she wasn't used to being swept off to magic places in private limos and planes.

His family, Bryant had told her, owned a house on the island, complete with private beach and housekeeping staff. It had been in his mother's family for over a hundred and fifty years and had once been a large and prosperous sugar cane plantation.

'I didn't know,' she'd said. 'You never told me.'

He'd given a faint smile. 'Ancient family history is not a subject that takes up priority space in my consciousness.'

The plantation house was a lovely place, white and gleaming amid luxuriant greenery. It looked like something straight out of a movie with its wide columned veranda with wicker furniture and flowering potted plants. Inside it was cool and airy, the wooden shutters open to allow in the sea breeze. Terracotta tile floors, wicker furniture and flowered fabrics in aqua and coral gave it a wonderful tropical feel. A big, comfortable bedroom was joined by a marble bathroom with fluffy towels and French toiletries. A friendly maid offered her help. Did the miss want her clothes ironed? Did the miss need a bath drawn? Did the miss want...?

A fairy-tale. Zoe smiled as she dug her toes in the soft sand, squinting against the bright glitter of the water. Bryant was coming out of the sea, emerging like a Greek god from the waves. The image made her chuckle. He looked wonderful, wearing nothing but black swimming-trunks, water streaming down his brown skin, his body sleek and fit. She watched the fluid movements of his body as he came toward her, enjoying the sight of him.

Washington seemed far away now, her worries no longer real. Bryant's lovemaking and the warmth of the sun had melted them away. There was no room for doubt or fear.

A thought occurred to her. Maybe Bryant had a plan. Maybe... She closed her eyes and swallowed as hope bubbled through her, as delicate as champagne. Maybe...

The thought was dangerously fragile, but elation and joy formed the words inside her head.

Maybe he's going to ask me to marry him.

He took her on a tour of the island for the rest of the day, showing her small villages and wonderful vistas and places where he had played as a child. They sampled the food he loved, eating at roadside stalls, drinking fiery ginger beer and sweet sorrel soda.

After they'd watched the pastel Caribbean sunset, he took her to a thatch-roof bar by the beach, dimly lit by kerosine lamps made from soda bottles. A huge Rastafarian in dreadlocks served them crusty, smoky jerk chicken. It was fiery, juicy and delicious and they drank copious amounts of Red-Stripe beer to cool the fires.

That night she slept curled up against him, his arms around her, dreaming lovely dreams. Tomorrow he'll ask me, she told herself over and over.

In the morning a champagne breakfast was brought to their room, wheeled in on a trolley covered with a shell-pink tablecloth. Zoe surveyed the luxurious display, taking in the sparkling silverware, the coffee-pot on a little brazier to keep it hot, the small bouquet of pink flowers, hot croissants, sliced fresh papaya and pineapple, and a bottle of champagne in an ice-bucket.

It was all a wonderful contrast to the rugged, rustic eating they had done the day before.

They ate and drank and laughed. They made love amid the croissant crumbs. It was wonderful. 'Ah, what luxury,' Zoe said afterward, stretching her legs, sipping champagne. 'I've never had champagne in the morning. It's truly decadent.'

Bryant grinned at her. She reached out and took his hand and played with his fingers.

'Tell me some of your other secrets,' she said softly.

His brows arched. 'Secrets?'

'Like this house, like the fact that you came here when you were a child and learned sailing and scuba-diving.'

'I have no secrets,' he said.

Her heart began a nervous, erratic rhythm. She buried her face against his neck. 'But there are many things you don't want to talk about,' she said quietly, and inside her a little voice called out a warning. Stop! Stop! Danger ahead!

'Not all subjects make pleasant topics of conversation,' he said lightly. He stroked her hair. 'Do you want to get up or would you rather sit in bed and read for a while?'

Side-tracked again. Actually, she was relieved, and the little voice inside her stilled. She didn't really want to talk about the forbidden—his wife, his marriage—and stir up old pains and unhappy memories. She didn't want to deal with the shadows in his eyes. Not now. Another time.

'I feel very lazy,' she said. 'Let's read.'

The *Sunday Post* not being available, Bryant settled himself against the pillows with the Saturday *Herald Tribune*. Zoe was not in the mood for contemplating the floods, famine and civil war that ravaged the planet, so she picked up a glossy travel magazine she'd taken with her from the plane. The photographs were gorgeous. She skimmed articles about the great hotels of the world, the best places to go scuba-diving, and then her eyes caught the travel story about Brazil.

Her heart skipped a beat. Brazil. Her gaze flew over

the lines, then she put her hand on Bryant's arm. 'Look, here, an article on Brazil.'

He glanced over. 'What does it say?'

'It's a travel story,' she said, trying to sound casual. 'What hotel, what beach, where to see jaguars and how not to get devoured by piranhas in the Amazon.' She put the magazine down. 'What's the latest on the proposal?' she asked, her heart suddenly thumping loudly, not knowing if she really wanted to know, feeling suddenly as if she'd put both feet into quicksand.

'We've made the short list and an inside contact told me we're the favorites to win the contract.' His gaze went back to the editorials he'd been reading.

She stared blindly at the magazine in front of her, the beauty of Brazil a blur of colors. She poured herself another cup of the strong Blue Mountain coffee and swallowed some with difficulty. Her stomach churned.

She'd been wrong, so terribly wrong. Hope had swept away her ability to see clearly, to recognize the signs. She had fooled herself. He wasn't going to ask her to come with him. He certainly wasn't going to ask her to marry him. This wonderful weekend was not meant to be anything but what it was—a wonderful weekend, an event in the present that had nothing to do with the future.

I can't go on this way, she thought. I've got to talk to him. Her hand shook as she put the coffee-cup down.

'Bryant?' Her voice sounded odd, as if it did not even come from her.

He glanced at her, frowning. 'What's wrong?'

'I want to ask you a question.' Be calm, she admonished herself. Do not fall to pieces.

He lowered the paper. 'What is it?'

She focussed on his bare chest. She loved that chest,

loved putting her cheek against it and hearing the solid beat of his heart. 'If your company wins the contract, you're planning to go to Brazil to head up the project, right?'

'Yes.'

Her hands were shaking and she hid them under the sheet. She heard the trill of a bird just outside the window, lovely and delicate. 'Do I in any way fit into your plans for the future? Are you considering at some point to ask me to come with you and Paul to Brazil?'

CHAPTER EIGHT

THE silence throbbed around them. It was the worst silence she had ever experienced, more eloquent than any words. It screamed in her head, shattering hopes and dreams. She slid her gaze from his chest to his chin, to the rest of his face. A strong, masculine face. A face she had touched and kissed intimately. A face that suddenly seemed alien and unreadable.

'You have a life in Washington,' he said then, his voice devoid of emotion. 'You have your cozy little nest, your job, your friends. You're settled as you'd planned to be.' His words came out calm and carefully measured. 'That's what you wanted, wasn't it?'

She felt a choking sensation. Not like this, she thought wildly. Not like this!

'It won't be the same without you,' she said, managing to look straight at him.

'I know,' he said, 'but I do have to leave.' He pushed the sheet away and got out of bed. Picking up a short robe from the chair, he put it on.

A pain stabbed her, sharp and brutal. He was retreating even now—getting out of bed, moving away from her. Those few steps symbolized a gaping void. She wanted to reach out and pull him back into bed beside her. She wanted to feel closeness and love and understanding. There was none there now and the beautiful, sunny room seemed suddenly hostile, the light too bright, stinging her eyes.

'You and Paul have become part of my life, Bryant.' How did she manage to sound so calm, so rational, when inside everything felt raw and ragged?

'Yes.' Curt, businesslike. He moved away even further, crossing the room, stopping in front of the open window, his back turned to her.

Rejection and anger and a whole mishmash of emotions twisted inside her as she stared at his back, knowing with a sense of hopeless inevitability that this was the end.

'I've become too...emotionally involved with you,' she said, dragging out the words. 'I don't think you really had that in mind, did you? You really don't want me to care that much.'

He did not respond. He stared out the window as if he had not heard her question. In the silence she could hear the soft swish of the waves.

Tears burned behind her eyes and she clenched her hands in her lap. 'I think we should break it off, Bryant.' It was not her voice speaking, not her body trembling. Oh, God, she prayed, please don't let this be happening to me.

For a moment he stood very still, then he turned to look at her, his eyes oddly dark. 'What is wrong with what we have right now?' he asked harshly. 'Why can't we enjoy it?'

She felt sick. 'Because it's not enough. Because...I...' Her voice cracked. 'Because I don't feel good about it any more.'

'What is it that makes you feel bad?' His voice was hard. He was a stranger, an angry stranger with cold blue eyes, and she felt her heart breaking.

'Bryant, please, let's just end it. Let's not make this worse than it needs to be.' She pushed her hair away from her face. She needed air. She needed to breathe.

'I want to know what makes you feel bad!' His jaw was rigid and his eyes held a cold blue fire.

She clenched her hands. 'I feel used.' So there, the words were out. Ugly words, leaving a bitter taste in her mouth.

'*Used*?' The word exploded into the room.

'I don't know another word,' she said helplessly. She raised her knees and hugged them to her as if defending or protecting herself. She felt trapped in this bed, this big, comfortable bed, still warm and rumpled from their lovemaking. 'You like being with me. Paul likes being with me. But I keep getting this feeling that, that…you're not taking it seriously. That it's a temporary thing and you enjoy it, but it's not…*important*.'

His jaws clenched. 'I didn't force you into this relationship.'

She winced at the words. 'No, you didn't. I entered into it out of my own free will and with my eyes wide open.'

Wide open but blind, she added silently.

She drew in a shaky breath. 'But I know now that I made a mistake,' she went on, forcing out the words. 'This relationship isn't what I need it to be and that's why I think I should get out. You don't really want…me…want me in your life.' Her voice almost failed her.

'You *are* in my life, dammit!'

'For the time being.' Until it's not convenient any more. She swallowed the thought.

'What do you want?' he said impatiently.

Anger clogged her throat. 'What do you want?' As if

she were asking for a pair of earrings he could run out and purchase to assuage her. She fought for a measure of calmness, forced herself to look him in the eye.

'Bryant, I am not asking you for anything. I don't *want* to have to ask. I only want what's offered freely.'

One brow arched, faintly imperious. 'And what I'm offering is not enough?'

'No.'

'What you want is marriage and children and all the rest.' His voice sounded vaguely disdainful, as if there were something unworthy about wanting marriage and children.

'No.'

'*No?*'

'No! I don't want marriage and children for the sake of having them. What I want is love and commitment, but I'm very well aware that that's not something you can ask for or demand or buy. I also know now that you haven't got them to offer.' Her voice broke and tears blurred her eyes. She took a shuddering breath. 'I'm sorry about that, but there's nothing I can do but accept it and deal with that reality. That's what I'm trying to do, in some sort of mature fashion.'

He jammed his hands into the pockets of his robe. 'How perfectly noble! How perfectly rational and logical! Well, I could have expected it! You and your well-organized life and your preconceived notions of how life should be lived! So I don't fulfill the fantasy you have of a doting husband and I don't fit into your comfortable domestic life. Haven't you ever heard of compromising? Of adjusting expectations? You're never going to find what you want, you know. You're lost in fantasy land. Let me tell you something, Zoe. Love and commitment isn't all that it's cracked up to be, and take it from someone who knows.' He stopped abruptly, strode into the bathroom and slammed the door.

His outburst left her shaking. It was not what she had expected—not the anger and emotion. She'd tried so hard to do this without offending him, without pressuring him, without angering him. Well, she had not succeeded. All her education and experience had not been enough.

To hell with my education! she thought furiously, throwing off the sheet and swinging her legs to the floor. To hell with Bryant Sinclair! What she wanted more than anything now was to rip open the bathroom door and shout and scream at him, hurt him as much as he'd hurt her. She wanted to beat and scratch his chest like some primitive cavewoman and rage at him until she would no longer feel the pain inside herself.

It was what she wanted to do deep down. It was not what she did, because, after all, she was no cavewoman.

On trembling legs, she dressed and gathered her things. She wanted to leave. There was nothing worse than being miserable in paradise. If only she could get to the airport in Kingston. She could get on a commercial flight and be home home by tonight. And spend the next several months paying off her credit card to pay for it. At the moment she didn't care. She caught sight of Bryant's car keys on the dresser, lying beside a jumble of bills and coins. She'd call from the airport and tell him where to pick up the car. With her heart racing, she picked up the keys.

The bathroom door opened and Bryant came out along with a cloud of steam and the scent of soap. He wore the short blue robe and his hair was wet from the shower.

His eyes met hers. 'Don't even think of it,' he said. 'I brought you here and I will get you back.' He reached out and took her hand and with a sense of futility she released the keys.

He put them back on the dresser, his eyes not leaving her face. 'I wasn't aware you felt used,' he said, his voice ragged at the edges.

She clenched her teeth. 'You make me feel that way. You make me feel that you're…interested in me because I'm available and convenient.' She laughed harshly. 'Available and convenient and ever willing. All you had to do was pick up the phone on Friday and I came running, not even knowing what you had in mind. I'm *pathetic*!'

'Zoe…' Something raw and painful flitted across his face, but she refused to let it affect her. He reached out and put his hands on her bare upper arms.

She froze. 'Don't,' she said thickly. 'Don't touch me, Bryant.'

Never before had she told him that and the words shivered between them like jagged shards of glass. His body tensed. All expression left his face and his eyes grew alien and distant. He released her arms.

'As you wish,' he said.

How she managed to spend the rest of the day without falling apart she would never know. The sun shone, the flowers bloomed, the birds chirped. Everything around her was beautiful and happy, mocking her misery.

Late that afternoon they boarded the plane and the hours stretched endlessly as they flew back to Washington. Occupying themselves with books and magazines, they spoke only when necessary, like polite strangers.

As she stared unseeingly at the magazine in front of her, the same questions kept repeating themselves in her mind over and over. What had possessed her to think that something would come of this relationship? What grand delusion had made her think a man like Bryant would want to marry her? A man who commanded the use of private planes, a man born to a wealthy family, heir to a large company.

She knew what had possessed her. Love. Love made everything possible, love made all dreams come true.

Love made you lose your mind.

It wasn't until she lay in her own bed in her own apartment late that night that the tears finally came.

The days stretched endlessly, stringing into an interminable week of sleepless nights. Much to her relief, Bryant still allowed Paul to come to her apartment after school, but when Bryant came home Paul went downstairs and she was left to have her dinner alone.

Once her apartment had seemed so cozy and warm and friendly. Now, without Bryant, it seemed cold and empty even though it was filled with lovely things to look at, sit on, read, touch—wall-hangings and carvings and leather poufs and large cushions and colorful paintings and a wall of books. She enjoyed them because they were interesting or pretty or comfortable. She enjoyed them, but they did not give her happiness. Surely on some level she'd always known that.

The problem with nests was that things alone weren't enough. It was the people you shared the nest with that made the difference.

'I've figured out what to do when I grow up,' Paul said importantly.

Zoe handed him a mug of hot chocolate. 'Great, tell me about it.'

The two of them had been home all day. The schools had been closed due to unexpected late March snow, which lay thick and white over the city. Paul had been out for hours with the kids in the neighborhood, playing and building a snow fort. He was in now, warming up and reading a book.

'I know what I wanna be,' he said. 'I wanna work with endangered animals, like in Africa or in Brazil in the Amazon. Kako and I have been writing about it and he wants to do the same thing. I've been reading about it in the book you gave me for Christmas and I've seen stuff on TV.'

'That's very important work,' she said.

He nodded soberly. 'We've gotta study a lot. Also, when I'm allowed to work, I wanna get a summer job in the zoo, to get used to it, you know.'

'Sounds like a good plan.'

'After high school I'm going to college to study about animals and stuff—what's it called again?'

'Zoology.'

He nodded. 'Yeah. Kako too. We wanna work together when we're big.'

He elaborated and she listened, intrigued. Obviously, he had given it a lot of thought. It was quite impressive. She felt happy to see the enthusiasm and the shine in his eyes. He'd not been happy lately, feeling upset about the changes in the relationship between her and Bryant and the fact that they no longer ate together at night and spent time together as a threesome.

'What did your dad say about your plan?'

Hesitation flickered in his eyes. 'I didn't tell him yet. I wanted to tell you first and see what you thought.'

She felt a warm glow. 'I think it's a wonderful plan, and you've really thought about it.'

His eyes were shining and his face turned faintly red. 'I think Dad will like it, too.'

'I'm sure he will.' Paul might change his mind a dozen times before he ever made it to college, but that did not matter. What mattered was that he had a goal, something to be enthusiastic about and work for.

He pointed at the book he was reading. 'This is really good. I'm almost finished. Then I'll go outside again and shovel the sidewalk.'

'I'll get started now,' said Zoe. 'I need some fresh air.' She'd been inside all day and she felt restless.

'I can come now too, if you want,' he said amicably. 'I can finish this later.'

'No problem. Just come when you're done.'

Zoe drank in the cold, clean air as she leaned on the shovel, taking a break after cleaning the snow off the front steps. She hadn't remembered how heavy snow was. Well, it was good exercise.

She needed to stay busy, not to think about Bryant. She needed to think about doing something new and exciting to keep her mind busy, to keep from hurting so much.

She moaned. She did not know how she was going to survive the next six months with Bryant living so close. Somehow she'd have to find a way. With more force than necessary she plowed the shovel into the snow. Stop thinking about Bryant. Stop thinking…

A taxi slithered to a halt in front of her and a woman came out, wearing a big, hooded fur jacket, bright red leggings and black boots. She had a small face with large, pale gray eyes. She held a gift-wrapped box in her leather-gloved hands.

'Excuse me,' she said to Zoe, her voice cool and slightly peremptory. 'Does Mr Sinclair live here?'

Zoe nodded. 'Yes, but he's not home right now.' She observed the beautiful face, the beauty mark on the left cheek, not knowing why she suddenly felt a strange uneasiness. Who was this woman? Two weeks ago she'd broken with Bryant and already here was another woman on his doorstep. Well, it was not her business, was it?

The woman frowned. 'I thought he'd be home because of the snow.'

Zoe tightened the scarf around her neck. 'A few inches of snow isn't going to keep him from doing what he wants to do.'

A glimmer of a smile curved the woman's mouth, but it did not warm her face. 'No, of course not. I should know that, shouldn't I?'

Zoe had no idea whether she should know that or not, but she assumed the question was intended to be rhetorical so she remained silent. There was something cold about that beautiful face that was disconcerting. She felt an odd sense of foreboding.

'Do you know when he'll be back?'

'About six,' she said automatically. It was when Bryant usually came home. 'Would you like me to give him a message?' She was, after all, a civilized, rational person. She could do this. She could be polite. She forced a smile. 'I'm his neighbor. I live upstairs.'

There was a short silence as the woman studied her. 'I'm Lauren, his wife,' she said.

CHAPTER NINE

BRYANT'S wife. Zoe's heart stopped. She could feel it stop. The breath stuck in her throat and her body froze. Then her heart began to thump wildly and her lungs sucked in the frigid air. Clenching her hands around the handle of the snow-shovel, she willed herself not to lose her composure. She forced herself to look the woman in the face.

'I'll tell him you were here.'

The woman smiled, but it didn't reach her eyes. They were curiously empty. 'Well, perhaps I can talk to Paul, then. I'd like to give him this. It's his birthday next week.'

Sirens went off in her head. Red lights flashing everywhere.

'Paul's not home, either,' she managed in a calm voice. 'He's at a friend's house.' It was even true. He was upstairs in her apartment.

And he'd come down and help her with the snow as soon as he'd finished reading his book. Panic rose to her head. She did not want him to come down and meet this woman claiming to be his mother.

She *was* his mother. She recognized the gray eyes from the photo, the beauty mark on her left cheek. A lock of black hair had escaped from the fur hood. It was definitely the woman in the photograph in Paul's room.

'If you like, I'll take it and give it to him when he

gets back,' she said, which was a lie. She'd give it to Bryant and let him decide what to do with it. She forced a smile. Her lips were stiff. Maybe from the cold. She shivered. 'It's getting colder by the minute,' she said conversationally. She didn't want this woman to see her discomfort.

The woman hesitated, a look of calculation in the hard eyes. 'I'll come back later. I'd like to give it to him myself. Thanks anyway.' She turned and slid back into the waiting taxi. 'Oh,' she said, before closing the door, 'would you mind telling Bryant I'll drop by his office in the next couple of days?'

Zoe nodded. 'I'll tell him.'

The woman slammed the door and the taxi eased away from the curb. Zoe began to shake with reaction as she stared after the car. As it rounded the corner, the front door opened and Paul came out, all bundled up against the cold.

'All done! Wow, I love this snow!' He reached for the shovel in her hands. He frowned. 'You look sick! Are you okay?'

'Just a little cold, that's all,' she managed.

'Go inside, then. I can finish this. Besides, we have only one shovel.'

'You do the sidewalk, then. I'll finish up the steps with the broom.' She suddenly had terrifying visions of the taxi returning, of the woman coming out and talking to Paul. Or worse. Men snatching him up and driving off with him. Oh, God, this was crazy. She closed her eyes for a moment and took a deep breath. Stop it! she told herself. Next she'd be imagining herself on the Oprah Winfrey show telling her sorry tale.

'I'm Lauren, his wife.' The words echoed in her mind as she finished cleaning outside, as she fixed two mugs of hot chocolate to warm them after they came back inside. They kept echoing as she watered her plants and cooked a pot of bean soup for her dinner.

She had assumed Bryant was divorced, but, thinking about it now, she did not remember him ever actually saying so. His wife had walked out on him when Paul was a baby, more then twelve years ago. But what had happened after that? He never told her. He didn't talk about his wife, ever.

There are always two sides to a story, she told herself. This was true, but she could not deny the fact that she had trouble believing that Lauren's side would generate any sympathy in her—not now, having met her today, having seen the cold, calculating look on the beautiful face. She shivered involuntarily.

She would have to tell Bryant that Lauren had come to see him and had wanted to see Paul. But she couldn't call him now at the office with Paul sitting right here. She'd have to wait until Bryant came home, call him and tell him to come upstairs, so that Paul would not hear them.

She was a nervous wreck by the time her bell rang twice as a signal that Bryant had arrived home and Paul could come down.

She gave him five minutes, then dialed his number with her heart in her throat.

'It's me,' she said when he answered. 'I need to speak to you in private. It's urgent.'

A short silence. 'What's wrong?'

'I can't talk to you over the phone. Come on up, and leave Paul downstairs. Lock the doors and tell him not to let anyone in.'

'Good God, Zoe! What the hell is going on?'

'Do what I say, will you?' She slammed the receiver down, her legs trembling.

He was at her door in seconds flat. 'What the hell is all this about?'

He looked so vibrant and alive, so utterly male, it made her heart race just seeing him. It made her heart ache with longing.

She took in a shaky breath. 'This afternoon, while I was outside shoveling snow, a woman came up in a taxi to see you. I don't think she thought you were expecting her.'

He frowned impatiently. 'Who?'

She swallowed hard. 'Your wife.'

'My *what*?'

'You heard me. Lauren, your wife.'

The color drained from his face. 'What kind of perverse joke is this?'

'No joke. It was her.'

He stared at her. 'How do you know? What did she look like?'

'She was short. Very pretty, with big gray eyes, black hair, and a beauty mark on her left cheek.' She indicated the exact spot with her finger on her own cheek. 'I saw a photo of her with Paul in his room that day I brought him home when he was sick.'

He closed his eyes briefly. 'Oh, my God. Where is she?'

'I don't know.'

'You don't *know*?' His voice exploded in the room.

'No, I don't know! She didn't tell me! She left in the taxi. She…she wanted to see Paul. I told her he wasn't home either, and all I could think of was to get her to leave before Paul would come down to help me with the snow.' She took in a deep breath. 'I don't know if he was supposed to see her or not. I was acting on instinct.'

'The last time he saw her he was three months old,' Bryant bit out.

'I wasn't sure.' She drew in a ragged breath. 'She said to tell you she'll see you in your office in a couple of days.'

His eyes lit up. 'Good. And she'd better be there, or I'll have her hunted down.' He moved to the door.

'She had a present for Paul, for his birthday, she said. She says she'll come back and give it to him then.'

'Like hell she will!' He strode to the door and opened it.

'Bryant?'

He turned. 'Yes?'

'What does she want?'

'I haven't got a clue, but whatever it is it isn't good.'

She forced down the fear that had haunted her for the last two hours. 'What if she wants Paul?'

He laughed harshly. 'Not a court in the land would give her custody, but in the meantime she could make plenty of trouble if she tried.' He walked out and Zoe leaned her head against the sofa and closed her eyes. A moment later the door opened again and he was back.

'Zoe?' Some of his color was back, but his face looked deadly tired.

'Yes?'

'Thank you. You did the right thing.' His eyes met hers and held them, and there was pain and grief and a mishmash of emotions she couldn't identify.

'I'm glad.' She was overwhelmed with the desire to go up to him, to put her arms around him and tell him she loved him, to tell him she would do anything to help him. Instead she sat silent and watched him leave again as a painful bitterness took over.

'I'm Lauren, his wife,' the voice echoed inside her.

Maybe they were not divorced. Was that why he had never wanted to talk about marriage with her? Because he was still married? But why would he be, after twelve years? It was crazy. It didn't make sense. And even if it was true, why hadn't he told her? Why hadn't he trusted her?

Life was so complicated. People were so complicated. Yet it was her business—people's lives and what they did with them. When it concerned other people it was one thing; she could be professional and objective. When it concerned herself or the people she loved, everything changed. She couldn't be objective. Her analyses and diagnoses were twisted and adulterated with huge doses of hope and expectations and dreams.

She couldn't trust her own thinking.

And what was more distressing yet was the fact that after all these months she really didn't know Bryant very well. All she knew was that she loved him.

She hardly slept that night, her mind preoccupied with thoughts of Bryant, of Lauren, and why she had come back. What did she want? What if they'd never been divorced? Fear curled around her heart, strangling. It consumed her through the night and through the next endless school day, and she was physically and emotionally exhausted by the time she came home.

'What's wrong?' Paul asked again. 'Are you sick? You were acting funny yesterday too and...' He stopped and frowned as if a thought had just occurred to him. 'Why was Dad here with you last night? He was acting funny too when he came down. What's going on?'

How did she answer that? She sat down, clutching the

teacup in her hands as if the warmth of it would give her strength.

'There are some problems, but they'll be straightened out. It's not for you to worry about, Paul. Just be a little patient.'

'But what is it?'

'It's big-people business. I know you don't like to hear that, but that's really all I can tell you.'

His face worked suddenly. 'I just wish we could go back to the way it was. I wish you and Dad...' He bit his lip. 'I'm sorry.'

'It's all right. I'm sorry about it too, Paul. We're all sorry, I think.'

She had a splitting headache suddenly. She had no strength for this conversation, no strength to deal with Paul's worries and pain, and it made her feel guilty. She got up from her chair.

'I'm going to take some aspirin. I'll feel better when my headache is gone.'

Paul went downstairs when Bryant came home and she ate her dinner and watched the news on television. Nothing but misery, it seemed. Civil war, a plane crash, murder and mayhem. Well, compared to that, her own life was not so bad after all. She grimaced. Cheer up, she told herself. You're doing just fine.

She wasn't doing fine. In spite of her exhaustion, sleep would not come and all she could think of was Bryant and Lauren and whether they were still married or not, whether that was the reason Bryant didn't want to commit to her. One thing was clear: she wasn't going to find out by thinking about it.

She'd have to ask Bryant.

He'd tell her his private life was none of her business.

She hesitated, but only briefly. She had nothing to lose.

She crawled out of bed, put on a long robe and warm slippers and grimaced at herself in the mirror. No need to get dressed, surely. Her courage might fail her by the time she was done, and she was covered up from the neckdown in blue cotton terry—hardly the stuff of romance and seduction.

She went down the stairs and knocked on his door. He opened it a moment later, a glass of brandy in one hand, his brows cocked in surprise.

'Not another crisis, I hope?' he asked mildly, stepping aside to let her in.

'I want to ask you something.' Her heart was pounding with nerves. She loved this man, had shared his bed, but he was a stranger now, a stranger whose thoughts and feelings she did not know.

He surveyed her. 'You're nervous,' he stated. 'Are you all right?'

No, she wanted to say, I'm not all right! She swallowed. 'I'm fine,' she lied.

He lifted the brandy glass in his hand. 'Would you like some?'

She nodded. Maybe it would help. False courage, but she'd take any courage she could get. He poured her a modest measure and she took a careful sip. It went down hot and fiery. She wasn't used to hard liquor, but it gave her a nice glow.

'Paul wanted to know what's going on,' she said, not quite ready to dive in with the real question. 'He's very observant and he knows something's wrong. I didn't tell him anything, of course, but I felt bad about it. He's worried.'

'Yes. We had a talk tonight. I think I was able to set his mind at ease.' He sounded cool and businesslike.

Had he told Paul his mother had been here? What had he ever told Paul about her? How did you tell a child that his mother had walked out on him when he was just a baby? She looked at Bryant's face, but his expression did not invite further questioning.

She took another sip of the brandy, aware of Bryant's eyes on her.

'What did you want to ask me?'

She cradled the glass in her hands, trying to stop the shaking. Gathering her courage, she met his eyes.

'About you and Lauren.'

His eyes narrowed. 'Yes?' he asked tersely.

She took a deep breath. 'Are you still married to her?'

He stared at her. 'Why the hell would I still be married to her? Of course I'm not married to her!'

She swallowed. 'I didn't know. You never mentioned it. And...and she said she was your wife.'

'She said she was my wife?' His tone was full of distaste.

She nodded. 'Yes.'

He laughed coldly. 'That was probably for your benefit.' He drained his glass and set it down. 'I divorced her years ago, which was no minor feat, let me tell you. It took me three years to find her.'

'I see.' She took a sip of brandy. She didn't know if she was relieved or upset. Obviously his marital status had not been the reason why he had not wanted her to be part of his life.

'Why do you want to know?' he said impatiently. 'What difference does it make now?'

Her throat ached. 'I'm just trying to understand you. I thought perhaps you never wanted to talk about us because you were still married, and the more I thought about it…' She rubbed her forehead. 'Oh, I don't know. I wished you could have trusted me with a little more of the important things in your life.' She felt tears come to her eyes. She was making a fool of herself. She was an emotional wreck. She didn't know what she was saying any more. Putting the empty glass on the table, she came to her feet. 'I'm sorry,' she said, her voice sounding unsteady. All she wanted now was to get out of there and be back in her own apartment.

She wasn't fast enough. He came toward her and then she felt his arms around her, turning her against him. His mouth came down on hers, kissing her deeply, hungrily.

Love and need flooded her, an ache so fierce she felt dizzy with it. She loved this man and she wanted nothing more than to be right here in his arms.

She loved him.

Not enough, came a whisper of thought. Not enough.

He held her tight against him, his hands roaming over her back. She felt his need and desire for her—his body, his touch, the soft groan that came from somewhere deep inside him.

Whispers of fear. Not enough. Not enough.

Please love me, she pleaded silently. Please love me.

A useless plea. Love wasn't something you could get by asking.

It took all her strength and every ounce of will-power she possessed to withdraw from him, to walk out through his door and close it behind her.

He called her at her office the next afternoon and her heart somersaulted as she heard his deep, familiar voice asking her if she had a moment.

Fortunately there was no one in her office. A girl with boyfriend trouble had just left. 'Yes, no problem,' Zoe said, wondering when, if ever, she would stop being so affected by the mere sound of his voice.

'Lauren was here,' he said.

'Nothing, there's nowhere for me to go, Zoe. And with no one to watch Paul, I can't start a new job anyway.' She wanted to scream at him, to break past this, to get to the next panel of the maze.

'Hush,' Wolfe said. He said—

CHAPTER TEN

ZOE'S hand clenched around the receiver and her body tensed. She closed her eyes, seeing the woman with the cold eyes in her mind, seeing her as clearly as if she stood right in front of her.

'She just left,' Bryant went on, 'and I thought I'd let you know she won't bother me and Paul again. Don't worry about her showing up at the door again.'

She felt relief sweep over her. 'What happened? What did she want?'

'She wasn't looking to take Paul away and sue for custody or visiting rights,' came his caustic voice. 'She wanted money.'

'*Money*?'

'It appears that her third husband left her nothing when he died a few months ago and she was thinking perhaps we could make a deal which might involve my giving her some "financial assistance", as she put it.'

'Why would you do that?'

'She thought perhaps I wouldn't want her to make my life and Paul's difficult. She had some very creative ideas about how she might accomplish that.'

Zoe grew cold. 'Blackmail,' she whispered.

'Loud and clear. Unfortunately for her, it's also loud and clear on a tape I had running to record whatever she might have to say to me. Just in case.'

Relief almost made her laugh. 'You are so clever.'

'We do what we have to do.'

'Yes.' She closed her eyes for a moment, his words echoing in her head. Last night she had left because she had to. 'Yes, we do, Bryant.'

He was silent for a moment. 'Well,' he said then, his voice crisp and impersonal, 'I thought I'd let you know.'

She'd been deep in thought and when Zoe reached the house she saw to her surprise that a man was sitting on the stone steps leading up to the front door.

A bearded man in jeans, dark, handsome, and with a devastating grin on his face as he saw her surprised face.

'Nick!' The breath stuck in her throat, then joy overwhelmed her. 'Nick!' she repeated and rushed up the steps straight into his outstretched arms. She hadn't recognized him right away; the beard had fooled her.

He'd always been a great hugger, and a warm embrace could not have come at a better time. It was like a balm for the empty feelings of loneliness she'd been struggling with.

'It's so good to see you,' she said, and her voice wobbled precariously. 'Oh, Nick, I'm so glad you're here!'

He put her away from him a little and grinned into her face. 'Do I see tears of joy?'

His face was blurry and she swallowed hard. 'Of course not! I'm smiling!' She smiled widely, threw her arms around his neck again and hugged him. 'I'm just so happy to see you! Good grief, that beard is funny.'

Then, across his shoulder, her gaze caught Bryant, eyes cool, keys in his hands. The warmth seeped out of her.

'I'm sorry to interrupt,' he said, 'but I'd like to get inside.'

Her heart sank, and she moved automatically to give

him access to the front door, pushing aside Nick's duffel bag. Bryant put the key in the lock, showing no sign of expecting introductions.

'Just leave it open,' she said; 'we're coming in.'

'As you wish.'

They followed him in, passing him as he glanced at his mail.

'My place is upstairs,' she said to Nick. 'Come on up.'

She didn't look down, but she could feel Bryant's eyes following them up the stairs.

'Good God,' said Nick as she unlocked her apartment door, 'that look on the guy's face was enough to freeze my blood.' He frowned at her. 'I thought you and he...'

'It's over,' she said, hoping he wouldn't ask more questions. He followed her inside. She took off her gloves and unwound her scarf, shaking out her hair. She watched him take in his surroundings.

'Great place,' he said. 'Very cozy. Just what I expected.'

'Why didn't you write and tell me you were coming?'

'I wanted to surprise you. I took my home leave early. My sister is getting married next week, in North Carolina. I thought I'd drop by and see you.'

She took off her coat and reached to take his jacket to hang it away. 'Can you stay for a few days? I don't have an extra room, but the couch is a sleeper.'

He gave a crooked smile. 'If you really, really want me to.'

'I really, really want you to,' she said solemnly. 'I'll even cook for you.'

'This is truly delectable,' Nick said, forking away his food with great appetite. In the past two days he'd found everything she'd concocted truly delectable.

'Thank you,' she said, and grinned. It was good to have company, to have someone to talk to and laugh with. Tonight, after they'd eaten, they were going to a party together. Had he not been here, she would probably have stayed home. She'd had little energy lately for things social. Not a good sign, she knew that.

'How's the travel bug holding out?' he asked, wiping his mouth with a napkin. 'Have you ever thought you might want to give up this life of comfort and abundance and go work overseas again in some poor and deprived place?'

She had. However, she was not thinking in terms of poor and deprived, but rather in terms of exotic and exciting. Ever since she'd broken up with Bryant, the idea had haunted her. She needed something new to excite her, a new challenge. Her nest-building aspirations had failed miserably. She had her nest, true enough, but it brought her no true happiness. It was a nice place to live. With a little effort and imagination you could have a nice place in Timbuktu.

Was she really meant to stay put here amid her pretty things and hope a man would show up one day and stay with her for good? It made her feel like a spider in a web, waiting for prey.

The image was not at all appealing.

It was no good to spend your life waiting for something to happen. It was better to go about what you really wanted to do, live a life that excited the heart and stimulated the brain cells; and if love was meant to happen, it would.

She looked at Nick and nodded. 'I've thought about it, yes. Why do you ask?'

He stroked his beard thoughtfully. 'Several reasons. For one, I don't think you're all that happy living here. You're just trying to make yourself believe you are. I sense a certain feeling of boredom and stagnation underlying all the surface enthusiasms you display about life in the nation's capital.'

She was silent. He was right, and it was amazing that he had sized her up so quickly, in a mere two days actually. Recognizing the truth had taken her a lot longer.

'Am I wrong?' he asked.

She shook her head. 'No.'

He took a drink of his wine. 'Also, I asked you that question because I have ulterior motives.'

'And what are those?'

'I've decided to see if I can persuade you to come back with me. I think we ought to stop all this loneliness nonsense and get married. We'll have each other and be happy forever.'

'You'll have to shave the beard.'

'I'll shave the beard.'

'I want breakfast in bed on Sundays.'

'I'll give you breakfast in bed on Sundays.'

She tilted her head. 'You'll have to stop being such a slob. I can't live with somebody who leaves his clothes and towels all over the house.'

'I'll stop being a slob.'

She bit her lip, trying not to laugh. 'Sure you will.'

'Marry me and I can do anything.'

She stared at him. 'Nick, you are not serious!'

'I'm very serious. You're my best friend. We laugh and have fun. It'll be great being married.'

She pushed her plate away and leaned her arms on the table. 'You're forgetting something.'

'And what is that?'

'We don't love each other.'

'Speak for yourself. I love you. Hand me the butter, will you?'

'Well, I love you, too.' She handed him the butter. 'But I don't think it's the right kind of love.'

'So what's the right kind of love? Look at what we have. We are great friends. We get along so well. We like the same things. We never fight. What more could you wish for?'

'Passion?'

He sighed. 'Passion is highly overrated.'

'Speak for yourself,' she said, trying to sound casual. A sudden fierce pain stabbed her.

He gave her a narrow-eyed look. 'Whenever I had passion, all the rest wasn't there and it invariably ended in disaster.'

'I'm greedy. I want it all.'

There was silence as he buttered a bread roll. 'The question is,' he said slowly, not looking at her, 'are you going to get it all?'

She couldn't swallow. She stared at the flowered tablecloth, seeing nothing.

The knife accidentally slipped from his hand and clattered against the plate. 'It's that arrogant bastard downstairs, isn't it? That iceberg?' There was an uncharacteristic note of anger in his voice.

She said nothing.

'You feel *passion* for *him*?'

She shoved her chair back. 'Oh, shut up, Nick!' She rushed into the kitchen.

He followed her in. 'What did he do to you?' he demanded.

She was gazing down at the bowl of fruit on the

counter, avoiding his eyes. 'Nothing. It was me. I expected too much. I wanted too much.' She swallowed painfully. 'I broke it off myself.'

'What did you want?'

She turned to face him, leaning her back against the counter. 'What did I want?' She laughed, a short laugh full of self-derision. 'I wanted him to want me in his life no matter what.'

'And he doesn't? Did he tell you that?'

'He's planning his life without me. He's going to Brazil on a long-term contract. He didn't discuss it with me and he didn't ask me to come along, nor did he ask what we should do about our relationship or anything. I just don't figure into it.'

He pulled her into his arms and guided her head on to his broad shoulder.

'Go ahead and cry,' he said. 'Although I must say I don't think he deserves your tears. He doesn't know a good thing when he sees it. Look at you—gorgeous, smart, loving. Will travel! Will cook! All that and passion too! Just imagine what a life he'd have!'

Oddly, tears did not come. 'Oh, be quiet, Nick,' she said thickly. She drew out of his embrace. 'Let's clean up this mess and go to the party.'

Zoe knew exactly when she stopped enjoying the party. It was the moment she looked at Nick across the room and knew he'd been drinking too much.

Oh, damn, she thought. Why didn't I pay more attention? Well, she wasn't his baby-sitter, was she? He was a grown man. A grown man with a problem, obviously. She called for a taxi.

'It's time to go home,' she said when it arrived ten minutes later. He said he didn't want to go. He made a joke and laughed. He wasn't funny. She took him by the arm and practically dragged him outside and pushed him into the waiting taxi.

He almost fell inside.

'You're mad at me,' he murmured accusingly.

'You're drunk and it's disgusting,' she said.

'You're right, is disgussing,' he said amicably. 'I'm a rotten sonoffabish.'

She gritted her teeth and looked outside, saying nothing. It had started to rain and drops dripped down the window. Fortunately it was not a long ride home and she was relieved when Nick managed to crawl out of the taxi on his own power. She paid the driver and he drove off.

Nick sat down heavily on the wet brick steps leading up to the front door.

'We need to go inside, Nick,' she said, wondering how she was going to manage getting him up the stairs. 'Stand up.'

'I wanna sit down.'

'I want you to stand up. It's cold, Nick, and you're sitting in the rain! For heaven's sake, don't act like a fool!'

He'd already been acting like a fool and she'd been embarrassed and mortified by his idiotic behavior. She was worried too. He liked his drink too much and that was not an encouraging sign. But right now, standing in the pouring rain, she felt anger building.

'If you don't stand up and try to get up the stairs, I'm going to have to find help! I can't just leave you here!'

'You stay with me, then. It's raining. I love rain. Rain brings life, you know that. Makes the desert bloom.'

'You'll freeze to death!' What was she doing, standing here arguing with an intoxicated male? She groaned.

She'd ask for help. She considered the possibilities. Maxie's husband was out of the country and no lights were on in her house; Maxie was still out or had already gone to bed. This left her with only one solution: she'd have to ask Bryant. Not a savory idea, but there it was.

She went inside the front door and knocked at his apartment door, feeling nervous and angry.

The door opened and he loomed over her. Surprise flickered in his eyes.

'I need help,' she said. 'Nick's outside. He's had too much to drink and I need help getting him up the stairs.' No sense in beating around the bush.

There was a pregnant silence. Bryant's eyebrows rose meaningfully and the rest of his features rearranged themselves in an expression of cool distaste.

'Nick, I assume, is that bearded character who's been staying with you?'

She gritted her teeth. 'Yes. He won't come up and if I leave him he'll freeze to death.'

Bryant's expression indicated that he did not find that a bad idea at all, but he made a move to come through the door and she stepped aside.

Without much ado, he hauled Nick to his feet and managed to get him inside the front door.

'You mus' be the guy making my Zoe unhappy,' Nick said, making efforts to stand up on his own power, and failing. 'Well, I tole her I'll make her happy. I'm gonna marry her.'

Bryant started shoving him up the stairs, saying nothing.

'She wans passion,' Nick muttered. 'I can give her los of passion. Whaddya think, can I give her los of passion?'

'Not now, you can't,' Bryant bit out.

'I'm gonna marry her. I love her. I always loved her, you know. I came alla way from Africa to get her.'

'Shut up,' said Bryant, his voice vicious.

'I always loved her...I jus' din't know it. For years I din't know it, and then she left.' He began to cry. 'If I'd told her I loved her she wouldn't have left. It was all 'cos of Bianca, my princess. She had bewitched me, this princess. You ever been bewitched by a princess?'

'Shut up!' said Bryant, and hauled him through the door of her apartment. Nick sagged down in a chair.

He turned to Zoe. 'What the hell is the matter with you?' he bit out, his eyes flashing.

'Nothing is the matter with me! There's something the matter with him! He drank too much!'

'And you have him shacking up with you! Are you crazy?'

Something snapped inside her. She put her hands on her hips and stared right back at his angry face. 'What business is it of yours? I can shack up with ten drunks if I want to! I can marry them all too if I want to!'

For a moment there was silence, her idiotic words hanging in the air between them. People said the stupidest things when they were mad, she thought. It was embarrassing. The anger left his face and his mouth, magically, quirked in a faint grin.

'Oh, but you wouldn't, now would you?' he said softly. 'Not at all your style, Zoe.'

'I asked for your help, not your criticism or analysis.'

'I don't find it very comforting that you have a sloppy drunk in your apartment. What's he going to do when he comes to?'

'Nothing. He's completely harmless, intoxicated or not.' Unfortunately, it wasn't the first time she'd seen him in this state.

'I'm not terribly reassured.'

'That's your problem.'

'So it is.' He held her gaze, and what she saw in his eyes made her heart flip over.

'Is this the guy who wrote that letter I saw?'

'Yes.'

'Are you sleeping with him? And don't tell me it's none of my business.'

'It's none of your business.'

'Goddammit, Zoe! What is the matter with you?'

'You're repeating yourself,' she said coolly. 'There's nothing the matter with me.' She opened the door demonstratively. 'Thank you for your help.'

Anger leaped in his eyes. He moved, pushed the door from her hands and closed it, his eyes not leaving her face. 'Are you sleeping with him?' he asked again.

'What's it to you whether I do or not?' she asked bitterly. 'Are you jealous? Well, get over it.'

'I wouldn't like to see you do something stupid.'

'I'm touched by your concern,' she said caustically, 'but may I remind you that you're not my keeper?'

Something flickered in his eyes. 'I care about you. Is that so strange?'

He cared about her. Bitterness filled her. 'No,' she said mockingly. 'Of course it's not strange. After all, I'm your neighbor, and your child's school counselor. Of course you care.'

'Stop it, dammit!' He moved forward and put his hands on her upper arms. He looked down into her face and he was so close, so dangerously close. His eyes were so blue and intense, she could not stand to look into them. She glanced away, feeling her legs tremble.

'Let go of me,' she said, but there was no conviction in her shaky voice. She closed her eyes.

'Not until you answer my question.'

She was suddenly too tired. It didn't matter. It was not important. 'No,' she said tonelessly. 'I'm not sleeping with him and I never have.'

'Good.' He let go of her.

She took a few steps back, away from him and the treacherous warmth of his body. She could have lied and told him yes, but playing games was not her style. It only complicated matters. She pushed her hair away from her face, still looking at him. He glanced down at Nick who hung in the chair like a sack of potatoes, his mouth open.

'Are you going to leave Don Juan in the chair?' Bryant asked.

She was tempted to, but decided to have at least a little mercy. She could imagine how bad he would feel in the morning. 'He sleeps on the sofa,' she said wearily. 'I've got to pull it out.'

A few minutes later Nick lay on the sofa bed, his clothes still on but his shoes off. He muttered something unintelligible, then became quiet.

Zoe looked at Bryant. 'Thank you.'

He made no move to go.

'You'd better go back down before Paul figures out you're gone,' she said pointedly.

'Paul's at my sister's in Philadelphia.' He looked straight into her eyes. 'I'm not leaving you here alone with him,' he said, his tone indicating that nothing she could say would change his mind. Yet she felt obliged at least to try.

'I'm fine, Bryant. He won't wake up until tomorrow morning.'

'I'm not leaving.'

She shrugged. 'Well, suit yourself. You can have the

chair. Goodnight; I'm going to bed.' She turned abruptly and her right leg connected hard with the metal corner of the sofa bed. She cried out and tears of pain sprang into her eyes. She lifted her long skirt to see the damage, but her black panty hose made it impossible to see.

'Oh, damn,' she said thickly, feeling as if she wanted to cry like a child over the pain. Cry because it hurt, cry because she felt miserable, cry for a thousand reasons.

'Are you all right?' Bryant made a move toward her.

'I'm fine!' A sob escaped her and tears ran down her cheeks. She rushed into the bedroom, hoisted up her skirt and stripped off the panty hose. Bryant was right behind her.

'Let me see.' He nudged her down on the side of the bed and went down on his haunches. Pulling her skirt up to her knees, she extended her right leg. Tears blurred her vision and she couldn't see a thing. She took a tissue and wiped her eyes, feeling his hand warm under her ankle as he lifted her leg slightly.

Some grazed skin, a sore red area. It would be one hell of a bruise tomorrow. She touched it gingerly with a finger and winced. 'I'll live.'

'I'll get you some ointment.' He went into the bathroom and came back with a little tube. He knew it was there—they'd used it once when Paul had cut himself. Gently he spread some on the grazed skin, and she watched him, feeling fresh tears slide down her face—not because of the physical pain but because of the careful, tender touch of his hand on her leg; because he was there, so close, so far, so hopelessly far.

'Does it hurt?'

'I'm all right.' She swallowed hard, but the tears kept flowing. 'I'm sorry.'

With a soft groan he sat down next to her and put his

arms around her, holding her tight. She closed her eyes and leaned into him, her face against the warmth of his neck. She felt him tremble—or was she imagining it?

It felt good, so good. She smelled the clean, familiar scent of him, sensed the warmth of his body against her own, felt his breathing quickening.

She had to get away. She had to tell him to leave. But the words would not come and her body did not move. There was the knowledge, deep and undeniable, that this was where she belonged, in his arms.

With a hand under her chin he lifted her face and searched for her mouth, sliding his lips across hers, tempting. 'Kiss me,' he whispered.

Her heart lurched and she felt herself begin to tremble. She slipped her arms around his back, opening her mouth to the warmth of his. Desire rushed through her blood, making her stir restlessly against him. She needed him. She wanted him. She didn't know if it was right or wrong. All she knew was that she loved him.

'Zoe?' His voice was a desperate, hungry whisper. His hands slipped under her blouse, caressing her breasts, flooding her with tingling warmth.

She couldn't think; she couldn't talk. A soft moan escaped her and the kiss exploded with fire and passion—a passion held in check too long. All was heat and desire and she clung to him, quivering, letting the magic sweep her away.

CHAPTER ELEVEN

WHISPERS in the dark. Hungry mouths, yearning hearts, desperate, searching hands. A frenzied dance of love and passion—fast, faster, ever faster. She was breathless, feverish with need.

Their clothes were gone, dropped on the floor. The room had been thrown into darkness when the light bulb had given out, as if on cue. Rain slashed against the window and the sound of it vaguely registered in her mind, then passed as all she heard was Bryant's breathing and the soft groan coming from deep in his throat. And the thudding of her own heart.

She loved him and she caressed his body, savoring the beauty and the strength of it, kissing him with a delirious urgency she'd never felt before. He did the same to her, making her body throb, sweeping her away into wild, turbulent rapture.

Eager, frantic loving. She clung to him as waves of sensation broke over her. She thought she would drown, but when the waves receded and the storm had calmed she was still breathing—alive, spent, replete.

He lay against her, heavy, damp, breathing hard, his legs entwined with hers. An endless, wordless time later, they slipped away from each other and slept.

In the morning she awoke, finding him next to her in bed, asleep. A rush of sweet emotion flooded her—love and tenderness and gratitude. This man was hers, this man who made her feel as no one ever had, this man whose kisses and caresses sent her senses reeling, whose whispered words were champagne for her heart.

She watched him sleep, seeing the regular rise and fall of his bare chest, longing to touch him, but not wanting to wake him. He looked at peace, his features relaxed, his thick blond hair falling over his forehead.

She wanted to wake up with him next to her in bed for the rest of her life.

He opened his eyes as if he'd felt her perusal. He stared at her for a moment, then closed his eyes again, draping a bare brown arm across his face. Under the sheet, Zoe searched for his other hand, but he slipped away from her grasp.

Her throat went dry.

He heaved himself upright and raked his fingers through his hair.

'I'm sorry,' he said tonelessly.

A cold hand squeezed her heart. Those were not the words that would make everything right, not the words she wanted to hear. She pushed her face into the pillow, closed her eyes, as if somehow it could take away the pain twisting through her.

What she had wanted was something dramatic, about how much he had missed her, how much he loved her. They'd get married tomorrow and work out their future together. Nothing mattered as long as she was part of his life.

She was a stupid, naïve romantic. She opened her eyes and pushed herself upright.

'Why are you sorry?' she asked, her voice sounding odd in her own ears.

He glanced at her then. 'Because it doesn't solve anything, dammit!'

Solve what? The problem that he couldn't give her what she wanted?

What she wanted was all of him. What she wanted was to hear him say, I love you. I want you with me always.

What she wanted was a fairy-tale, a dream, a fantasy, and obviously nothing of the sort was forthcoming.

It was pathetic, truly pathetic, that she couldn't stop dreaming. She should go on with her life and forget this debacle, this pathetic game of self-delusion.

From somewhere she found a reserve of strength, strength to stay calm, to go on breathing. She forced herself to look into his eyes. 'Don't apologize. I didn't tell you no.'

She saw the hard line of his jaw, saw anger flashing in his eyes, bright as fire.

'Why the hell didn't you?' he ground out.

Her throat felt raw and painful. 'You know why, Bryant.' She slipped out of bed, put on a robe and walked out of the room. She'd wanted him because she loved him, in spite of everything. Because for that short period of time she could forget the despair and only feel the happiness, the joy of being in his arms, the joy of loving him.

In the bathroom she took a deep breath and willed herself not to cry. She had a quick shower, dried off and put her robe back on. Looking in the mirror, she saw the dull look in her eyes and grimaced. On with life. Grit your teeth. This too shall pass, she told herself.

In the living-room Nick was sitting up on the side of the sofa bed with his head in his hands. Actually, he was sagging more than sitting—the picture of misery and pain.

All she'd ever wanted was one man in her apartment.

One man who loved her passionately and was ready to commit himself to her and their relationship.

Well, here she was, not with one, but with two men in her apartment, both of them wanting her, each in his own way. One of them, suffering from a hangover, wanted to marry her, but had no true passion to offer. The other was ready to offer her passion temporarily but had no commitment in mind for the long term.

If only she could take them apart and reassemble them so that at least she'd end up with the right man and the right qualities in one body. She grimaced wryly and went to the kitchen to brew a big pot of very strong coffee.

Ten minutes later Bryant strode into the living-room, dressed, looking tall and in command. Nick stared at him. 'What the hell are you doing here?' he demanded.

Bryant looked at him as if he were a repulsive bug and remained loftily silent as if it was not worth his energy to reply.

Nick glanced at Zoe. 'What's he doing here?' he repeated.

'He helped me get you up the stairs last night,' she said, somewhat evasively. 'You had a bit of trouble with your legs.'

Nick closed his eyes and groaned. 'God, I'm sorry, Zoe. I don't know what got into me—'

'Booze got into you,' cut in Bryant coldly. 'After I dragged you upstairs last night, I thought it might be prudent to stay around in case you got any funny ideas in your deplorable state of inebriation.' His tone was caustic.

Nick groaned again and looked pleadingly at Zoe. 'I don't think he likes me,' he said. 'Have I ever as much as laid a finger on you in all the years we've known each other?'

Zoe sighed. 'No, you haven't, Nick.'

He looked up at Bryant looming over him. 'I'm really a good guy. I can even talk big like you when my head doesn't ache.'

Zoe handed him a cup of coffee. 'Drink this. I'll get you some aspirin.' She glanced over at Bryant. 'Care for a cup of coffee?'

'No. I'm leaving.'

Such a happy gathering it was.

Bryant left. Nick crawled, moaning, back under the covers. Zoe went shopping.

She spent hours shopping. When she arrived home, Nick was up. The bed was pushed back, the living-room reassembled, and his duffel bag stood packed by the door.

'The family awaits me,' he said, 'and I must bid you farewell.'

'You weren't leaving until tomorrow,' she stated.

He nodded. 'I think I'd better leave today. I am terribly sorry for my disgraceful behavior. I think it's time for me to admit that I had better stay off the stuff completely. I don't seem to know when enough is enough.'

'Yes.'

He gave her a crooked smile. 'No recriminations? No lectures? No advice?'

She shook her head. 'There's nothing I need to tell you that you don't already know.'

His eyes held hers for a long moment. There was sadness there, and regret. 'That guy downstairs is a moron,' he said roughly. Then he put his arms around her, hugged her, and left.

* * *

Zoe heard the news at school, from Ann, who had acquired the information through the grapevine, along which it had traveled in a rather circuitous route. It did not surprise Zoe to hear the news from Ann, knowing Ann, and knowing how small a world Washington really was, and how well-developed and powerful the grapevine.

Bryant was going to Brazil. His company had won the contract and he was going to take charge of the project.

She felt a mixture of emotions—fear, despair and a terrible sense of inevitability. If she had nursed any secret hope at all, there was none left now. And there was anger. It was none of her business, but she could not deny she was angry—angry because it became obvious that Paul knew nothing of his father's plans.

Bryant was planning to move overseas for a number of years and he hadn't even told his son. She could not believe it. It was unthinkable.

In a few months, Bryant and Paul would be gone for good. There had always been the secret hope that the project would fall through, that his company would not win the contract, that Bryant would stay...

She tried hard not to fall apart. Falling apart was embarrassing and undignified and got in the way of things. She kept herself busy, doing anything and everything she could think of to get her mind off Bryant and her feelings for him. She had a couple of small dinner parties. She signed up for a Spanish class. However, although determined to avoid a total breakdown, she did allow herself to cry at night—she might as well, because she was going to cry whether she wanted to or not. Crying was a useful tool—it relieved anxiety and stress. It would help to get him out of her system. Maybe. Oh, God, she didn't know.

The awful thing was that he was so close—just one flight of stairs down. All she'd have to do was walk through his door, put her arms around him and tell him she didn't care about tomorrow, that all she wanted was to be with him now.

It would be a lie. She did care about what happened tomorrow and, no matter how great the temptation, her sanity won out every time. She might be a romantic and given to enjoy things sensual, but she knew the value of common sense, the value of pride, and the value of not selling yourself short.

Maybe it had been inevitable. Zoe stared at the application forms in front of her. Next to them lay several copies of her résumé.

You could not force fate.

All she'd been thinking about lately was leaving, finding a job overseas, finding new stimulation and adventure.

She glanced around the room. She'd wanted to come home and grow roots. So why was she dying to get on a plane again?

I'm not meant to have roots, she thought. I have wings.

She was not a plant with roots in the soil, but a bird with wings. She smiled suddenly. The image pleased her. Her mind produced a picture of a bird with bright-colored feathers singing lustily from a tree branch high, high above the ground.

Spring once again gave it a try. The temperature rose, the buds swelled some more, birds chirped louder. In the spirit of cooperation, Zoe too tried to feel the promise of a new beginning. After all, she was working on her own new beginning, having sent off application forms to various far corners of the globe.

In truth, she was happy about going overseas again. It was the right thing for her. However, there was another truth, one that caused no happiness at all. It caused her sleepless nights and a pain in her heart that did not want to go away: she could not stop loving Bryant.

Every time she caught a glimpse of him, getting out of his car, or leaving for work, she felt her heart turn over. Once she'd come home from her Spanish class and standing in the entryway she'd heard his voice behind his door as he'd called out something to Paul. She'd stood there, aching with such need and longing, it had frightened her. She'd run up the stairs and, sitting on the couch in her own apartment, she'd hugged herself and rocked while tears streamed down her facc.

She knew that leaving would not make the pain go away. It would go with her wherever she was.

One day, fate, or perhaps simple coincidence, had them collecting their mail together in the front hall. Bryant acknowledged her presence with a polite nod, then directed his attention to the stack of paper from his box, riffling through it quickly.

Zoe took her own mail, giving him a quick, sideways glance, catching the frown on his face. His eyes were trained on a large envelope. He raised his gaze, giving her an odd look. 'This is for you,' he said, handing her the envelope.

She took it from him, seeing her name clearly on it. Apparently the mail man had put it in Bryant's box by mistake. It was from the international employment agency she had contacted for a job, its logo big and colorful on the top left-hand corner.

'Looking for a job overseas?' he asked casually as he glanced through his mail.

'Yes.'

'I thought you were planning to settle here.'

'That's what I thought too. I intended to, but I changed my mind.'

He glanced up the stairs. 'You have a special place.'

'It's only a place to live.' How matter-of-fact it sounded. How very true it was.

He met her eyes. 'I thought it was more than that.'

She was silent. At one time it had been, but no more. She felt no comfort there now, no sense of safety.

'It's only a place to live,' she said again. 'I've decided I'd rather explore the world some more.'

He glanced down at a small padded package in his hand. 'Where are you planning to go?' he asked casually.

'I've applied to schools in Thailand, Malaysia and Paraguay,' she answered in her most businesslike voice.

'Food's best in Thailand.'

Fire and spice. She felt a stab of pain, remembering what he had written in the cookbook he had given her for Christmas. 'For the woman who gives me fire and spice and everything nice.'

He'd made the comment on purpose, she was sure. 'Yes,' she said calmly, determined not to show him her feelings.

He put the key in the lock of his door. 'Well, good luck.'

'Thank you.' It was all so polite and civilized. That was all there was left. She wished being with him weren't so painful.

'Good luck', he had wished her. Maybe it helped, she thought a few weeks later as she read the letter from

Malaysia. It certainly was good luck that she had a job offer so soon. Malaysia. She read the letter and the accompanying information with mounting excitement. They wanted her! It was wonderful!

She rushed out to the library that same evening, finding more books. She'd already read general information about the countries where she had applied, but now it was time for more serious research.

She arrived home with a load of books, struggling to find her key, cursing herself for not having brought a bag to carry the books. A car stopped. Bryant appeared by her side.

'Let me get it,' he said, but he was too late. The books slipped to the ground.

'Oh, damn,' she muttered, and went down on her haunches to pick up the books. He helped her gather them, his body and face close to hers. She smelled the familiar scent of him, felt a terrible pain sear her heart, sensed rather than saw the tension in him as he gave her back the books.

He took his key and opened the front door.

'Thanks,' she said huskily.

'Going to Malaysia?' he asked casually, looking meaningfully at the stack of books in her arms.

'Yes. I have a job offer. I thought I'd get myself informed before I left.'

'Very commendable.' His voice was curiously flat. He put his key in the door of his apartment.

Her heart began a nervous dance in her chest. 'I heard through the grapevine that your company won the contract and that you're going to Brazil,' she heard herself say. She'd been determined not to ask him about it, but here she was, doing it just the same. She clutched the books against her chest. 'Paul doesn't know anything about it, does he? Why haven't you told him?'

He arched a brow. 'How do you know what I tell my son or not?'

'If he knew you'd be moving to Brazil, he would have told me! We're friends, Bryant. He confides in me.' Her throat closed. He spends hours at my apartment. I love your son, Bryant, she added silently. She drew in a careful breath. 'I think it's irresponsible to make these plans and not include him some way, not even *tell* him!'

He put his hand up on the doorpost and eyed her narrowly. 'The reason why I haven't told him, Counselor, is because we're not going.'

It took a moment for the words to sink in, a long moment to find her tongue. She stared at him, not knowing what to think.

'You're not going? What do you mean?'

He turned to face her, one brow cocked. 'I mean what I said. I'm not going to Brazil. I turned down the job.'

Her heart began to beat frantically. 'I thought you wanted that job. I thought you couldn't wait to get out of here.'

He nodded. 'True.'

'Then why?'

'Because of Paul. I decided that you were right, Counselor. He's happy here and I don't want to take the chance of having things fall apart again. Contrary to what you seem to think, my son is more important than my work.'

'Yes, yes, of course.'

Oh, God, she was such an idiot, such a presumptuous idiot. She'd been ready with her opinion knowing only half the truth. It was embarrassing.

A smile tugged at the corner of his mouth as he studied her. 'Did you really think I would knowingly do something that was not in my son's best interest?'

'I...no, of course not. You just didn't seem to think that it was wrong. You seemed to think he could make the adjustments this time.'

'Well, I had time to think about it, and I reconsidered.'

She swallowed. 'Well, I'm glad. I think you're doing the right thing.' She turned and walked up the stairs, holding on to the books for dear life, feeling like a fool.

Two days later he called her on the phone. 'Checking to see if you're home. Can we talk?'

'When? Now?'

'Yes, but not on the phone.'

'Fine, come on up.' She'd started sorting through her possessions in preparation for her eventual departure. The room was a mess, the floor covered with piles of books and various decorative items.

She told him to come in when she heard his knock on the door. She was down on her knees packing books in a box.

He stared at her, at the empty shelves, the piles of books. Something flickered in his eyes. 'What are you doing?'

'Sorting through my things. I want to get organized so I can ship my stuff as soon as possible. When I get to Malaysia I don't want to have to wait for months to get it.' She took another stack of books and positioned them in the box. 'When school here is out I'm going to Italy to stay with my mother until my new job starts.'

He stood very still, his face taut, as he looked at her. Something lurked in his eyes—something dark and wild—and suddenly the room seemed filled with a shivering tension.

'You're serious about leaving,' he said, his voice toneless. It was a statement, not a question.

'Yes, of course I am. I have a new job.'

He raked his hand through his hair. 'We'll miss you.'

'You'll get over it,' she said coolly, feeling annoyance take over her sense of unease.

His eyes seemed to explode with anger. 'Goddammit, Zoe! Why? Why do you have to do this?'

Her body tensed at the tone of his voice. She clenched her hands into fists in automatic defense. 'Do what?'

'Leave the country!'

She shrugged, trying not to feel affected by his anger, to stay calm. 'Because I want to. I want a new adventure and I'm free to do what I like to do.'

In one swift movement, he picked up a box of books and flung the contents across the floor. 'I don't want you to leave, dammit!'

Her heart pounded against her ribs and she stared at him in shock. His eyes were a deep blue, flaming with angry desperation. There were any number of things she could say, but nothing came out of her mouth. He stood close, looming over her.

'I want you home! Here! In this place! I want to know that Paul has a place to come home to! I want to know you're here when I...' He stopped abruptly, turned on his heel, strode out of the door and slammed it.

She was shaking. She slumped, hugging herself, closing her eyes.

Silence.

Then the throbbing of her heart, and the drone of an airplane high in the sky. She smelled dust, and the fresh scent of spring greenery wafting through the window.

A memory, a voice, flitted through her head. 'I came

home from work one day and found her packing.' Oh, God.

She sat on the floor amid the scattered books and ravaged dreams, not moving, his voice still ringing in her ears. He didn't want her to leave. He wanted her right here.

He cared. His outburst had shown her that, and the look of raw despair as he'd seen her sitting amid her possessions, packing—not just packing up her things, but packing up his world. He had known. And he had cared.

It wasn't enough.

She had no desire to serve as a convenience to him. She had her own life to live and her own dreams to dream.

Footsteps outside her apartment. The door flew open and he was back, his face tight and unreadable. Her heart leaped into her throat. He shoved his hands into his pockets and met her eyes.

'Please stay,' he said roughly.

Her whole body tensed. Everything inside her screamed to tell him yes, she would stay. But something else was stronger, fighting, struggling. She felt as if she was teetering on the edge of an abyss. Her heart was pounding and her whole body was shaking. She looked right into his eyes, feeling panic rise, forcing it down.

'No,' she said.

CHAPTER TWELVE

BRYANT stared at her, frozen, silent.

Time seemed to stretch. Zoe noticed the wine-red color of his shirt, the rise and fall of his chest underneath. She heard a car coming down the street, the cooing of a pigeon near the open window. From somewhere came the voices of children. Small sights and sounds. Insignificant details of ordinary living.

She felt a terrible sense of inevitability. In her mind she heard the tortured sound of her own voice. *No.* If he walked out now, everything would be lost.

He did not walk out.

She watched his feet coming toward her, as if in slow motion. He knelt down beside her on the floor and took her hands. 'Zoe,' he said hoarsely, 'please, please don't leave me.'

His eyes were so blue, so blue. She looked into their depths, mesmerized, hearing the echo of his words. 'Don't leave me'. She saw his lips move, making more words.

'I can't bear the thought of you not being in my life. Marry me. Please marry me.'

She hadn't heard it. It was a trick of her imagination. She had so longed for those words that she was now hearing them in her mind.

'What?' she whispered, afraid to breathe.

'I love you. I want to marry you.' He took her face in his hands. 'I love you, Zoe,' he said huskily.

Hot tears flooded her eyes. She dragged in a breath of air and felt herself begin to tremble, felt something inside her begin to crumble—a great big wall of fear and pain and anger. And then she was crying, big heaving sobs she couldn't stop. With a groan he wrapped her up in his arms, rocking her.

'I'm sorry,' he whispered, 'I'm sorry. I didn't mean to make you cry.' He wiped her tears, kissed her eyes, her mouth. 'I love you,' he said again.

'I...didn't...know.' She fought for control, willing herself to stop crying. 'You...you wouldn't let me close. Sometimes you seemed so far away.'

His face worked. 'I know. I know. I didn't want to admit that I needed you in my life, that I needed any woman in my life.' He paused, eyes closed, struggling with himself, with his words. She felt his breath warm on her cheek. His arms tightened around her. 'And then I came in and saw you kneeling there, packing up, getting ready to leave, and...and something inside me went crazy.'

She heard again the thud of books scattering around the room, saw again the raw panic in his face.

'I know,' she whispered. 'You thought of the day you came home and found your wife packing.'

'Yes.' He groaned, then straightened slightly, gathering courage. 'And after I walked out here I stood at the top of the stairs, looking down, and all I saw was a dark, bottomless void, and I knew I couldn't go down, because there was nothing there, nothing at all.' He rubbed his temple. 'And as I stood there it came to me that you weren't packing up to leave me, but that I had left you long before.'

She swallowed at the constriction in her throat, saying nothing, letting him talk.

'I realized that you're nothing like Lauren, that you had given me all I ever wanted, all the things she never had—warmth and joy and love; that you were giving me the priceless gift of being a mother to my son. And I stood there looking at that blackness, knowing I was throwing it all away.' He closed his eyes again. 'Oh, God,' he muttered, and fiercely put his mouth on hers as if to imprint her with the truth of his words, as if to make sure she was there with him, real and solid in his arms.

'Marry me. Stay with me.'

'I will,' she whispered. 'I will.' She clung to him, overwhelmed with love and a dizzying relief.

'You're all I ever want,' he said against her mouth. 'I want you with me, at the table, in bed, in the same house. For the rest of my life.'

A lightness spread through her, tingling like champagne, rising to her head. She felt like singing and dancing and laughing. 'Oh, Bryant, I love you so.' She kissed him with a sudden wild abandon, fiercely, passionately.

They made love on the floor amid the jumble of books. It was wild and wonderful and full of primitive delight, exorcising the past, celebrating the future.

'What about your new job? About going to Malaysia?' Bryant asked. He'd poured them a glass of wine and they'd toasted their new life together, still sitting naked on the floor, looking for all the world like the survivors of a hurricane. 'You really wanted that.'

Zoe felt a fleeting sense of regret, quickly gone. 'Yes, but I want you more. You and Paul are infinitely more important.'

'You wanted the excitement and challenges of a new place,' he went on. 'Would you have liked to go to Brazil?'

'Yes, of course I would have. But we can't leave now because of Paul, and that's all right. It isn't the place, you know. It's the people.' She paused for a moment, looking into his eyes. 'I want to be where you are, or for you to be where I am. The place doesn't matter.' She gestured around. 'I wasn't happy here because this was such a nice apartment, or because Washington was such a wonderful city. I was happy because you and Paul were here with me.'

He smiled a little, playing with her hair. 'You made this a very special place.'

She spread her fingers out on his chest. 'But in the final analysis it's only a place. It's only things. What made it special was that we were in it together.'

He took her hand and kissed her palm. 'We'll buy a house and you can put your talents to work and make us a nest out of it again. A love-nest.'

'Yes,' she whispered.

'And when the time is right we'll all go overseas again for a new adventure. And we'll live in whatever place we can have and you'll make it into a love-nest again. Promise?'

She nodded. 'I promise. Wherever we are, I'll make us a nest.'

He stroked her thigh, a blue glimmer of humor in his eyes. 'What if there's no electricity or running water?'

She glowered at him. 'Don't push me.'

They were putting books back on the shelves, looking prim and proper and fully dressed again, when Paul knocked on the door a while later. He'd been to the movies with some friends and Bryant had left a note on the door telling him to come up to Zoe's apartment when he came home.

Zoe was looking forward to seeing his expression when he heard about their plans, and she was not prepared for his angry face when she opened the door. His hands were clenched by his side and his eyes shot fire.

'What's wrong?' she asked, alarmed. She stepped aside to let him in and he stormed past her, stopping in front of his father. 'You should have told me!' he blurted out. 'Why didn't you tell me?'

Bryant's eyebrows shot up. 'Tell you what?'

'About Brazil! They wanted you to go to *Brazil* and you said no! Why didn't you tell me? You never told me! You never said anything about it!'

Surprise flitted across Bryant's face. 'Since when do I discuss my career decisions with you, Paul? Why are you so upset?'

'It's my life too!' Paul stood straight, his eyes blazing up at Bryant who towered over him.

'I considered your interests, Paul,' he said quietly.

'Well, you should've asked me because you considered wrong!'

Zoe could tell that Bryant did not appreciate Paul's tone of voice, but was doing his best to contain his anger for the moment.

'This concerned my work and my career. We're talking about a complicated, adult issue and consulting you was not appropriate. I'm the adult and you are the child.'

'I'm not a child! You think I don't understand anything! You think…' He was shaking with anger. 'Well, I do understand! You don't wanna go because of me!'

'Why do you say that?'

'Because it's true! You were always planning to go

some other place again! You told me so! And now you changed your mind!'

'For a good reason. Sit down, Paul.' Bryant sat down next to Zoe on the couch.

Paul dropped on to a carved African stool, looking mutinous.

Bryant leaned forward, hands dangling between his knees. 'Paul, I decided it's better for us to stay here for a while. You like your school and you've settled nicely and there's no need to go overseas again so soon and have to start over with a new school and all the rest.'

Paul's head snapped up, his eyes pleading. 'Dad, don't you understand? I *want* to go! I want to go to Brazil! *Brazil*, Dad! Think about it!'

Bryant's brows lifted fractionally. 'Why do you want to go to Brazil?'

Paul gave his father an incredulous look. 'The Amazon, Dad! The Pantanal! The animals! Think of all the stuff I could see and learn! Don't you understand? It would be awesome!'

For a moment Bryant was silent. 'I'm trying to do what's best for you,' he said then. 'You had a hard time adjusting when we came here. You were unhappy and lonely and I don't think we need to go through that again.'

'We won't! Dad, I'm *thirteen* now! And you and I understand each other, and...' he swallowed and glanced over at Zoe '...and Zoe has taught me a lot about feelings and stuff and...' His voice faded, his eyes lost their angry spark and sadness dulled them. 'Zoe isn't staying here, Dad. She's leaving.'

Bryant's face softened as he looked at his son. 'No, she's not, Paul. She changed her mind. She'll stay here with us.'

Paul looked at Zoe, then back at Bryant, his face a study in surprise. He swallowed visibly. 'You mean...'

Bryant's mouth quirked. He put his arm around Zoe. 'Yes. We've decided to get married. I hope it's all right with you.'

Paul's face turned red, his eyes grew bright and for a moment he was speechless. Then his body went into motion, doing an Indian war dance accompanied by a loud whooping. He collapsed on the floor. 'This is awesome!' he said, panting. 'This is so cool! I can't believe it!'

He lay still, catching his breath. Then suddenly, with a surge of new energy, he leaped to his feet and looked quickly from Zoe back to Bryant.

'I've got it! I've got it all figured out! We can all go to Brazil! I won't have any problems at all, don't you see, Dad? I'm gonna have my own personal counselor in the house!'

Zoe laughed and looked at Bryant, who rolled his eyes heavenward. Paul turned his excited gaze to her.

'You wanna go, don't you? I mean, you *told* me you wanna go some place again!'

'I did tell you that, yes,' she said carefully, 'but it's something that needs to be discussed.'

'Discuss it, then! Tell Dad you want to go! Discuss it so he'll say yes! Then it's two out of three!' He took a gulp of air. 'You want me to leave?'

'Yes,' said Bryant.

Paul rushed out the door. 'I'll sit on the stairs. Just call when you're done. Just hurry up!'

The door closed with a bang and Zoe swallowed a laugh. Bryant looked at her, eyebrows cocked.

'What do you suggest we do, Counselor?'

She bit her lip. 'You're his father.'

His eyes did not leave hers. 'And you'll be his mother.'

She swallowed. 'I suggest we go to Brazil.'

'You told me clearly and specifically that it would be a very irresponsible thing to do.'

She waved away his words with a casual gesture. 'That was because you were going to go without me as your personal in-house counselor,' she said, and grinned.

He scowled. 'I don't want you here or anywhere else as my personal counselor. I want you as my wife and don't you ever make a mistake about it.'

'Okay,' she said amicably, and kissed his cheek.

'What about Paul?' he asked. 'Will he be all right?'

'I think he pleaded his case very eloquently. And besides, he's much, much older now than last year.' She gave him a solemn look and he groaned.

'I'm having a terrible vision.'

'What's that?'

'The two of you together, ganging up on me for the rest of my life.'

She smiled winningly, running her finger lazily down his shirt-covered chest. 'Well, you wouldn't want to be bored, would you?'

He drew her close against him, putting his mouth on hers. 'Not a chance of that. With you it's fire and spice, all the way.' He lifted his face so that he could look into her eyes and gave her a devilish grin. 'I like it.'

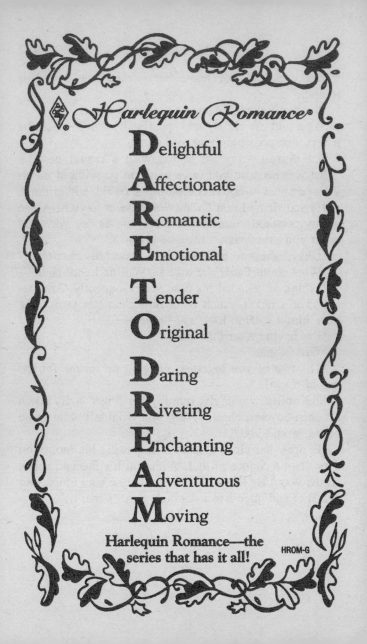

Harlequin Romance®

Delightful

Affectionate

Romantic

Emotional

Tender

Original

Daring

Riveting

Enchanting

Adventurous

Moving

Harlequin Romance—the
series that has it all!

HROM-G

Harlequin®
Historical

From rugged lawmen and
valiant knights to defiant heiresses
and spirited frontierswomen,
Harlequin Historicals will
capture your imagination with
their dramatic scope, passion
and adventure.

Harlequin Historicals...
they're too good to miss!

HARLEQUIN®
I N T R I G U E ®

We'll leave you breathless!

If you've been looking for thrilling tales of
contemporary passion and sensuous love stories
with taut, edge-of-the-seat suspense—
then you'll *love* **Harlequin Intrigue!**

Every month, you'll meet four new heroes
who are guaranteed to make your spine tingle
and your pulse pound. With them you'll enter
into the exciting world of Harlequin Intrigue—
where your life is on the line
and so is your heart!

THAT'S INTRIGUE—DYNAMIC ROMANCE AT ITS BEST!

HARLEQUIN®

I N T R I G U E ®

INT-GENR

LOOK FOR OUR FOUR FABULOUS MEN!

Each month some of today's bestselling authors bring
four new fabulous men to Harlequin American Romance.
Whether they're rebel ranchers, millionaire power brokers
or sexy single dads, they're all gallant princes—and
they're all ready to sweep you into lighthearted fantasies
and contemporary fairy tales where anything is possible
and where all your dreams come true!

You don't even have to make a wish...
Harlequin American Romance will grant your every desire!

Look for Harlequin American Romance
wherever Harlequin books are sold!

HARLEQUIN SUPERROMANCE®

...there's more to the story!

Superromance. A *big* satisfying read about unforget-
table characters. Each month we offer
four very different stories that range from family
drama to adventure and mystery, from highly emotional stories to romantic comedies—and
much more! Stories about people you'll
believe in and care about. Stories too
compelling to put down....

Our authors are among today's *best* romance writ-
ers. You'll find familiar names and
talented newcomers. Many of them are
award winners—and you'll see why!

If you want the biggest and best
in romance fiction, you'll get it
from Superromance!

Available wherever Harlequin books are sold.

◆ HARLEQUIN®

Not The Same Old Story!

 HARLEQUIN ◆ PRESENTS®

Exciting, glamorous romance stories that take readers around the world.

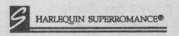 *Harlequin Romance®*

Sparkling, fresh and tender love stories that bring you pure romance.

HARLEQUIN® *Temptation*

Bold and adventurous—Temptation is strong women, bad boys, great sex!

 HARLEQUIN SUPERROMANCE®

Provocative and realistic stories that celebrate life and love.

 AMERICAN ◆ ROMANCE®

Contemporary fairy tales—where anything is possible and where dreams come true.

HARLEQUIN® INTRIGUE®

Heart-stopping, suspenseful adventures that combine the best of romance and mystery.

 LOVE & LAUGHTER™

Humorous and romantic stories that capture the lighter side of love.